Mountain High,

Valley Low

RENEE FLAGLER

Aspicomm BOOKS

A Division of Aspicomm Media

Published by Aspicomm Books
A Division of Aspicomm Media, Inc.
PO Box 1212
Baldwin, NY 11510

ISBN 0-9760466-0-1
Library of Congress Control Number 2004094700

This novel is a work of fiction. Names, characters, places and incidents are a product of the author's imagination. Any resemblance to actual persons, living or dead, places, events or locales are strictly coincidental and intended to provide the fiction work with a sense of authenticity.

Printed in the United States of America

For Les, Milan and the Daniels Clan.

Acknowledgements

Nothing happens by accident; therefore I must first give thanks to my Savior for making everything possible. Thank you for my gifts and guidance.

Special thanks to my editors, Susan Herriott and Quamin Ellis. Thank you, Brian Walker, for exceptional work with the cover design and layout.

Thanks to my family and friends for unwavering support and absolute confidence in my abilities: my husband, Les, my little star, Milan, and my mother, Eva. To Cora, Valorie, Patricia, Eileen, LaShawn, Jereema, Dana and Lori, thank you for believing in me.

I wish to acknowledge two authors whom I greatly respect, Barbara Rogan and Darren Coleman. Thank you for your insight and encouragement.

I would like to thank those who have gone before me to pave the way. I appreciate all you have done.

Lexie   CHAPTER I

My new office was larger than my bedroom. It came fully furnished with a breathtaking view of the East River through massive floor-to-ceiling windows. In the center of the floor stood an impressive charcoal and black glass top desk and a black meticulously designed leather chair. Beautiful contemporary art adorned the walls.

Just thinking about the fact that this was my new office made my head spin. I was completely startled when Shari, the loud-mouthed, homegirl, administrative assistant came up behind me to confirm that I would be meeting with the big bosses today. I wondered how she always knew the happenings before everyone else did. I assumed she was screwing one of the VPs. I was almost sure of it because she always received privileged information before anyone else. People say white men secretly love black women. I still figured they would be turned off by her somewhat ghetto disposition, but apparently they aren't.

I received the promotion of a lifetime: Alexia Mitchell Director of Marketing and Business Development. They had the nerve to ask if I would be interested in taking the position. I wanted to say, "What do you think, I'd rather stay where I am in my little office with no windows and blow the chance of receiving a seventy-five percent salary increase, perks up the asshole and an expense account to boot?" I simply swallowed, flashed a winning smile and gaily stated, "I would be honored." I managed that much while muffling the scream that slowly rose in my throat. It took all of my energy to contain my desire to break out in a chorus of "Go Lexie, it's your birthday!" right in front of the crew of VPs at the conference table. All but two were white and only one was a woman–Mary Ann–who would be my new boss. Arthur, the only black male, fit all of the stereotypical requirements that an Ivy League black man is expected to meet in order to make it in the big corporate arena. He was fairly good-looking with a nice medium brown complexion. He had perfect white teeth, an MBA from Columbia and an annoying voice. I am almost sure he had a snowflake snuggly tucked away in his wallet as the icing on the cake. However, I must admit the brother did know his job and there are not many that could match his abilities. He pretended to barely notice the sisters in the office unless they held certain positions. I often wondered if he showed more interest in white women because it "looked good" for his image. I've caught him staring hungrily at Shari's backside every now and then, but I was sure he wouldn't be caught dead with "Ms. Thing" in public. Surely it would be bad for the image and probably his pockets. Shari was not only very ghetto but increasingly high-maintenance.

I stood in my new office–with a view–as the new Director of Marketing and Business Development, deciding whom to call first. I knew my mom would be proud even though she thought I would have been more successful as a lawyer, probably because it would have been easier for her to explain my success in more common terms. My two sisters and I didn't grow up with much, and we were all determined to make it big. I decided to call them first. Dionne was "Ms. Black America." She had big goals, attitude and status. She was well on her way to the good life with the right job, the right money, and the right man. Ava was well-educated, married with children and happy as a pig in poop. I decided to conference them both.

"All right, spit it out," commanded Dionne.

"Yeah girl, I can't wait. I know it's something big," coaxed Ava.

"What makes you two think it's something big?" I teased.

"Maybe from the way you were screeching and whispering at the same time," Dionne said

"You think?" I joked.

"Oh come on already – I can't wait! What is it?" Ava blurted.

"Okay ladies, you are speaking to the new Director of Marketing and Business Development of Comtel Communications." Dionne and Ava screamed just like when we were kids. I felt so proud.

"I am so happy for you girl," Ava said

"You better go, girl!" sang Dionne.

"I'm trying."

"Now you know we have to go out and celebrate." Dionne suggested we all go to the 21 Club the following Friday night.

"Sounds good to me," I agreed.

"Ava sweetie do you think the hubby will let you out of his arms for a few hours just to hang out with your sisters?" Dionne teased.

"Hush, I would never miss this. My baby sister is moving on up in the world," Ava beamed. "Well I have to get back to work. I'll be there, just tell me the time. Did you tell Mama and David yet?"

"Not yet."

"What about Brooke?" Dionne asked.

Brooke was my best friend since kindergarten. We have been

inseparable ever since. We were so much alike yet so different in many ways, but we truly clicked. Brooke was the type of girl that you never knew what would come out her mouth next. She was anything but predictable. "I can call Brooke now if you ever get off of my phone," I teased.

"Well, see-ya-later-bye," they said together.

I couldn't wait to get to David's house to tell him the news. I wanted to tell him in person. When I got there I used my key to get in. David was sitting on the couch listening to Najee with his eyes closed. The music filled the room like a quiet storm. I slammed the door hard, startling him.

"Girl you need to be careful. You can get your head blown off like that!"

David teased as he sat looking as fine as ever in drawstring sweats, bare feet and no shirt. His chiseled cocoa-brown body was just calling my name. I stood for a moment studying his physique. From his long, jet-black eyelashes to his sculptured face complete with deep dimples and luscious full lips, all the way down to the bulge he couldn't hide even when he wasn't excited. David had the kind of eyelashes that made women jealous. All the mascara in the world wouldn't make my lashes look that good. David knew I was studying him and he had the sudden urge to stretch and show himself off. I blurted out the details of my day fast enough to just get it out and get on with other things.

"Get outta here!" David said. He was clearly excited for me.

"Who's the woman, baby?"

"You are *the* woman, baby girl. You know, something told me not to leave you today," he teased.

"You're a mess David. I am so happy."

"I'm happy for you."

David embraced me as I snuggled my nose in the center of his neck. He let his hands slide down my side and we held hands, fingers entwined.

"Are you sweetie?" I asked.

"Of course, I know how much something like this means to you. I'm proud of you." David smiled revealing a perfect set of beautifully white teeth set between two succulently fleshy lips.

"I love you, David."

"Yeah?"

"Yes, I do."

"Well you know, I never 'beat up on' an executive before," David teased, using our code phrase for wild and passionate sex.

"Oh really?" I quizzed raising a brow.

"Really."

David licked those lips causing the muscles within my vaginal walls to twinge.

"So what are you saying?" I inquired as heat rose along my back.

"What do you think?" David's smirk sent a tender streak of pleasure through the center of my being.

"You wanna beat it up a little, huh?" I teased, stepping back from David, preparing for his next move.

"Executive style." He licked his lips again. My knees almost gave out. Damn those lips.

"Executive style, huh?"

I almost lost my composure.

"Yes, let me show you." David pulled me to him slowly holding my face in his hands and planted soft kisses all over my face, leaving moist luscious imprints of his full lips. David proceeded to kiss and caress me gingerly, exploring my body with the tips of his fingers. He nearly drove me into an erotic frenzy before lifting me into his arms, carrying me to the bed and making passionate love to me for what seemed like hours. David brought the session to a close with a soft warm kiss.

"Did you enjoy your stay?" he teased.

"Why yes I did."

"Do come again."

"I intend to."

"Okay, now get out. My girl should be home any minute."

David burst out in laughter, and this time I beat him up for real.

Brian   Chapter 2

I have always wondered why the phone only seems to ring when you really don't feel like talking to anyone. The only reason I answered is because it could have been my mom.

"Hello."

"Hello Brian!" Shelly hailed in her cheerful tone.

"Hi Shelly." *Why did I answer the phone?* I made a mental note to call the telephone company and get caller ID.

"Hey sweetie, I haven't heard from you in a while," she said.

That's because I didn't want to speak to you. "Yeah, well I have been pretty busy. I am working on developing some new programs for a job." *Maybe I could just change to an unlisted number.*

"Well can't you take a little break?"

"I really have a lot on my plate right now. How about we get together another time?" I said. I really didn't feel like being bothered with her tonight.

"Oh come on. I'm sure you deserve it. You have probably been sitting in that house all week working on that project. I'm coming over. I'll cook you some dinner. I know you probably didn't eat. Besides I can try out something I learned from the Food Network."

"Shelly..." *But you can't cook!*

"No. I don't mind. I need to see you anyway honey, please."

"But Sh…"

"Just give me twenty minutes. See you soon, cutie. Bye!"

Damn, I can never get a chance to say no to that girl. Shelly is fine but she talks too damn much, mostly about herself. Okay what's wrong with her? Not much besides the fact that she is a pain in the ass. She means well. She's fine. She's got a nice ass, a tight body, and nice hair. She's sweet in bed. But, she's a royal pain in the ass. She can't cook but she often tries. I have to find a nice way to get rid of that girl before she starts to really get hooked. I have tried almost everything but blatant disrespect, and that's just not me. For some reason, she has in her mind that we have a future. She just doesn't understand that we are not for each other or at least she is not for me. Before I knew it she was ringing my damn bell. Reluctantly I opened the door.

"Brian sweetie, look at you, you look like you could use some TLC. It's a good thing I called."

Shelly brushed past me hurriedly heading towards the kitchen. She began removing groceries from her bags to set out on the counter. Not once did she pause long enough to take a breath. I tried to stop her for her lung's sake.

"Shel…"

Shelly held up both hands motioning for me to say no more and headed in my direction.

"How about I run a nice hot bath for you, put on some Kenny G. or something and you can relax while I prepare you a nice little dinner." Shelly placed her hands on my shoulder and spun me towards the bathroom. She took me by the hand to lead me through the house. I lagged behind like a child not wanting to go to church on Sunday.

Suddenly I halted in my tracks causing Shelly to turn her attention back to me. I surrendered my hand to the air.

"That sounds cool. I'll take care of the bath myself. You just go to the kitchen and I'll catch up with you when I'm done."

I needed to get away from her. I pointed in the direction of the kitchen. Shelly crossed her arms across her chest and threw me an inquisitive stare.

"Okay, sweetie, you take your bath while I prepare your dinner. Trust me. You'll love it."

Before I could respond, Shelly spun and dashed back to the kitchen, her words trailing behind her.

"Enjoy your bath honey. I'll see you in a few."

After soaking for about an hour I heard Shelly summoning me.

"Brian"

"What do you want Shelly?"

"Dinner's ready. I know you are going to love it. It's lemon basil chicken and vegetables." Shelly was visibly proud of her work.

"Interesting." I wondered how this was going to turn out.

"I've got the table all set up. Hurry up sweetie," she hastened.

"I'm coming."

The bath was just what I needed. I just hoped the food tasted decent. I had plenty of stress to relieve because of the project I was working on, and I knew this was just a bootie call with some extras.

"Um, baby, doesn't it look delicious? I can't wait to taste it," Shelly said proudly checking out her edible masterpiece.

Shelly really did a nice job setting up the table. There were candles, a vase with a single rose in the center and a bottle of Chardonnay. The food actually looked good, but I've been here before with Shelly and looks had been deceiving.

"Yeah, it does look all right." I braced myself for the expected.

"Okay honey, wait. Let's dig in together," Shelly said, giddy with pride.

I cut a piece of the chicken, dipped it into the sauce for a little flavoring and put it in my mouth. I felt my senses dull. Something was incredibly wrong. I could see it in Shelly's face that she tasted the same thing I tasted. The chicken was so salty it felt like the salt severed my tongue. We sat there for minutes with our mouths gaping open, refusing to taste or speak. I closed my mouth when I felt saliva making its way down my lip. I grabbed a napkin and got the chicken out of my mouth. Shelly followed suit. Together we devoured our glasses of wine to exonerate the bad taste. I drank so fast I lost breath. Still unable to utter a word, we simply laughed. We laughed so hard we both ended up in tears.

"So much for the delectable lemon basil chicken," Shelly continued to laugh with tears streaming down her soft cheeks.

"How much salt did you put in the chicken Shelly?"

"The recipe said, apply generously," she sputtered through her laughter.

"You need not be so generous next time." We burst out laughing all over again.

"Really sweetie I am sorry, I tried," She said wearing an expression of faux pity.

"Don't worry. You'll make up for it I'm sure."

And she did, all night long.

When I woke the next morning, I secretly hoped to find her long gone. I realized my wish hadn't come true when I saw her sexy body curled up on the opposite side of my king size bed. Maybe she'll be gone by the time I finished jogging. I threw on a pair of sweat pants, a t-shirt, turtleneck and a hooded sweatshirt to guard myself against the frosty air of late February. I was thankful the winter was finally coming to and end. I anticipated everything new the spring season had to offer.

I had an insurmountable amount of work to complete in order to be prepared for the upcoming Data Technology trade show the following week. I looked forward to four days in sunny LA. The women in L.A. were fine as hell and damn near naked. I try not to mix business with pleasure, but in L.A. you just couldn't help it. Besides, I had grown tired of the single life and longed for a woman with intelligence and a nice body. My past was beset with nothing less than the most problematic women God had ever created, plagued with varying cases of psychosis.

11

I thought of myself as a calamity magnet because I often attracted problematic women like Donna. She had three kids and two baby-daddies. When she got pissed off I couldn't tell when she was talking to herself, the person inside her head or me. We hadn't even kissed and she was telling people she was my fiancé. She couldn't hold a job and she was just looking for love in all the wrong places. Then there was Elise. She's kind of woman that constantly reminds you what a good catch she is. She travels the world. She speaks three languages; English, French and Italian. She acquired an MBA from John Hopkins University and holds a high position at the bank. She also has a bad attitude, and bad back teeth, which causes bad breath. But she is fine.

Finally there is Lori. Lori is down to earth. We could talk all night long, hang out, get busy, listen to music, watch the game together or whatever. No strings attached. No jealousy. No commitments. No problem. We clicked. The problem with her is she has a bigger fear of commitment than any man out there. Lori and I could not see or speak to each other for weeks but once we got together you would never know. It was like Lori was one of 'the boys.' The difference was, she had breasts and something real sweet going on between those legs of hers. But as far as Lori and I being together, that isn't going to happen. We don't want to lose the friendship we have and we're both cool with that. As far as sex is concerned she was my safety net. Kind of like "break into ass in case of emergency." Lori would call me and say, "Yo, B, what's up? I need a tune up." I'd say, "Give me fifteen," and we would end up screwing the house down, watching a game, drinking beer and eating some pizza.

As I get older, my interests are leaning more towards a nice normal woman that I can share my successes with. Call me corny, but I want something real. Until then I'll be married to my career.

When I returned, Shelly was standing in the entrance to my home office with a long black see through robe hanging open, black lace half bra holding up her ample breasts, black sheer thong, a garter belt, thigh highs and black patent leather pumps. She had a bottle of wine in one hand and two flutes in the other. Her body looked like melted caramel. My man betrayed my interest and stood at attention. It was time to make Shelly call on the name of the Lord once again. After that I needed to find a way to get her out of my place.

Lexie   CHAPTER 3

"David, come on! I'm going to miss my flight!" I yelled at him, knowing it was my own fault for running late.

"I'm waiting for you," David said.

"Okay, okay. I'm coming. Get my bag please." I snickered at the thought of why I was running late.

"I'll wait for you in the car, Lexie." David gathered my red   13
Kenneth Cole luggage and headed for the car.

I had less than an hour to get to JFK for my flight. I don't know where the time went. I could have sworn that I started out on time. This was going to be my first time in LA. I had a meeting first thing in the morning with software specialists at the Los Angeles Convention Center for a special project I was heading. This could be a huge win for me at work.

David leaned back into the door and yelled, "Lexie baby, you're going to miss your flight. Let's go!"

"Here I am. Help me out a little baby. Do I have everything?" I took one last look around the living room to make sure I hadn't left anything behind.

"Lexie, you've checked your bags ten times already. If you don't have it, you don't need it."

"Damn baby, you trying to get rid of me or something?"

I smirked and David rolled his eyes.

"You want to miss your flight?" David was firm.

"Oh, of course not. I'm coming."

I grabbed my coat and purse off of the couch and checked once again for my house keys.

"So let's go. You were the one complaining about missing the flight."

David headed back to the idling car outside.

"Relax baby, I'm coming." I took another look around, hopped through the door and locked it behind me.

Traffic was thick in spells. When it became clear at certain points, David drove so fast I could hardly speak. My right leg was sore from jamming my invisible breaks on the passenger side. I was running late but I did want to get there alive. Once we made it there safely, I kissed David goodbye and he practically kicked me out to the curb. I looked up and saw the time. It was twenty minutes before my flight to L.A. was scheduled to depart. I still had to check my bags and rush through the terminal to catch my flight. The ticket counter was jammed packed. I spotted a stout white man with one of those little Jewish beanie things on his head staring hungrily at my breasts and legs. I said what the hell and approached him since he was so close to the front of the line. A woman's got to do what a woman's got to do! He smiled. I winked. His smile broadened. I straightened my back so that the curve of my breast commanded his attention. He turned red. I started to walk towards him. He looked like he was going to burst into flames. He smiled from ear to ear.

"Excuse me, but I am awfully late and I am afraid I am going to miss my flight. If you don't mi..."

He jumped in, "No problem. Here take my spot. I am a little early." Now smiling like some kind of buffoon he stepped aside and gave me his place in line. A woman behind us sucked air and sighed.

"Thank you ever so much." I licked my lips and asked, "How can I repay you." I thought he was going to pass out. I started looking for a pacemaker.

"No... Don't worry. It's my pleasure darling," he said.

"Why thank you." I raised my breast one more time gave him a little shake then sashayed my ass over to the ticket agent shouting "Next." It's a good thing I had on one of my fine Donna Karan power suits. I didn't want to be mistaken for a high-priced whore. Mamma always said, "A real woman can be all things. She just needs to know what to be at a given time, and things will always work in her favor."

I looked at the ticket agent's mouth moving but heard none of what came out. I was stunned.

"You mean to tell me that even though I have a booking that this flight is full and there is no way I can get on!"

"I'm sorry ma'am, but you are very late. I can place you on standby for the next three flights; however as of now they are all booked solid. The next flight that I can guarantee you a seat on departs at four o'clock p.m."

I was heated, and quite sure that I didn't clearly get all of what she had just said.

I asked, "What time is the next flight for which you can guarantee me a seat?"

"We are booked solid until four o'clock. I can..."

"FOUR O'CLOCK IN THE AFTERNOON!" I dropped my

carry on and felt my palm cover my forehead.

"Yes ma'am." She eased back from the counter.

"It's only ten in the morning. What am I supposed to do until four this afternoon?" By now I had both hands on the ticket counter. I looked as if I could take it in one leap.

"I am sorry ma'am. I can put you on standby for the flights before and confirm you for the four o'clock flight, but that is all I can do for you now. If you like, I can go ahead and set you up for first class at no extra charge."

Damn, damn, damn! "Okay, I have no choice. I'll take it. Thank you." I couldn't believe this. What the hell am I supposed to do until four o'clock in the afternoon? I had no intention of sitting in the airport for the next five to six hours.

I pulled out my cell phone and called the office. I made up a fake emergency story about getting to the airport late and let them know that I was unable to make my flight but I would be on the four o'clock flight this afternoon. The truth about my lateness was that I had to get some "fine tuning" before leaving. Knowing I was going to be away for the next couple of days, I backed David up in the shower this morning to get a piece of him to take with me for as long as it would last. Just thinking about it made me shudder. If anyone saw me they would only think I caught a chill.

What the hell was I to do for the next five hours? I called Brooke to chew the fat for a few but she was at work and had to go. It was only a little after eleven in the morning. David didn't live far from the airport so I called his house knowing he should have been back by now. No answer! I dialed his cell phone. No answer! Shit! I grabbed a cab to David's place figuring I could go there for a while and put my bags down, take care of some business and make a few

16

calls. I wasn't sure if he was going to work from home or go into the office. David worked for a small record company and didn't work normal business hours glued to a desk and computer. He spent a lot of time working from home and being on the road. His company sent him all over the city and the tri-state area. I tried his cell number one more time, still no answer. I thought that was odd because he used that phone for business, and it was always on even when he was at home. I figured maybe in the midst of our rushing this morning that he may have left it at home.

When I got to David's condo there was a Silver Navigator parked in his secondary spot next to his Benz. I assumed he was with someone regarding work. I put my key in the lock expecting to hear them talking, instead I heard nothing. I eased in attempting not to disturb him and placed my bags down in the foyer. That's when I heard noises coming from David's home office, which sounded as if he was pacing around on the telephone like he usually does. I knew he was alone because David did all his business in the living room. He very rarely allowed anyone in his office. That was his space. As far as he knew, I was on my way to L.A. for the Data Technology Conference, so I decided to treat him to a little surprise. I quietly removed my clothes only to remain in red matching thong, skin-toned thigh-hi stockings and red stiletto pumps. I tiptoed to the fridge and found the whipped cream and sprayed small creamy circles around my perky nipples. I knew just how I wanted to make good use of my waiting time. I sashayed to the door of the office and kicked it in like I was Clint Eastwood about to do some damage, and I froze.

I saw a woman's thick, naked behind hiked up on David's computer desk. Her ratty weave was long and wild. Her head was thrown back with her legs were straight up in the air like the letter "V." Between those thick hairy legs was my David, jamming himself in and out of this woman like he owned her. One of his hands cupped her small breast while the other cupped her big behind. Both of them were breathing so wildly neither of them realized I was standing there. I felt my senses dissipate. I stood frozen, breasts hanging, cream dripping, temples tightening. My head swirled. Before I knew it I was screaming like a mad woman. I had completely lost all the good sense I was born with.

"Bastard!" I shouted.

David's cheating ass was shocked and so was his whore-bitch. David's eyes widened like half dollar coins and his tongue nearly hung to his chest. I thought David's tongue was going to fall out of his mouth. I threw the can of whip cream at them and charged for them. David moved away from the woman so fast he nearly dropped her. He tried his best to restrain me from ripping his balls from between his legs.

"Lexie! What are you doing here?"

The woman was in a state of shock and didn't know whether to make a run for the door or jump out of the window.

"WHAT THE HELL DO YOU MEAN, WHAT AM I DOING HERE!" I shouted.

"You were supposed to be on your way to L.A."

David was facing me holding my arms to keep me from snatching his manhood away. He stood with his mid section further away from me than the rest of his body.

"Convenient for you, right, you cheating bastard? You couldn't wait until I left, could you? Could you David? You bastard, I am going to kill you!"

I charged at him and he grabbed my arms to protect himself from my wrath.

"Wait a minute, Lexie. Baby wait!" he said

"Oh no you didn't, no you did not just call me "baby," have you lost your mind?"

With that last comment I freed myself of his hold and charged for what used to be my lil' buddy.

"Oh shit! Lexie, what are you doing?"

David's legs tightened trying to protect his little buddy between them.

"Screw you! I will snatch your balls right from between your legs, bronze them and hang then on the wall!"

I was wild with fury. The look in David's eyes said that he didn't know this crazy, naked woman with breasts hanging in front of him trying to castrate and bronze his balls.

"Lexie, baby, let me explain," David pleaded covering his manhood with one hand and tried to keep me aloof with the other.

"Explain! What is there to explain! I walk in and catch you in here with another woman and you want to explain. What else could you possibly explain that I couldn't figure out for myself? What are you going to explain that I didn't see what I just saw?"

David was dumbfounded and the woman was still frozen naked in the same spot. I whirled around and stormed out of the room in search of something I could use to beat the shit out of both of them. David must have known what was on my mind because he came running after me.

"Let me explain, Lexie. Baby, let me explain!" he pleaded again.

I raced towards the kitchen and pulled a stainless steel frying pan from the overhead rack. Just as I got the frying pan down, David reached the kitchen and looked at me in horror. I went after him with the pan held high in the air like a lunatic. My breasts were still loosely bouncing, dried cream streaks stained my abdomen, thong, stockings, and heels. David ducked and ran out of the kitchen towards the living room. When he reached the hallway, the woman ran her naked dumbfounded ass out of the office with her clothes haphazardly gathered in both hands. She held them close to her ample body. I began to chase after her. Both of their dumb asses were running around the living room like idiots bumping into each other trying to get away from me, still naked. She managed to make her way to the front door and I went after her. She tripped and fell over my bags in the hallway. Ass was everywhere! She managed to get up and shoot for the door before I could get to her. David took that opportunity to run back towards the bedroom.

Still naked, she ran out the house and jumped her jiggling ass into the silver Navigator. I ran out the front door after her as she began to pull out of the spot. I hurled the frying pan at the truck and smashed the front windshield. She pulled back and peeled out, leaving behind the screech of her tires and skid marks in place. Luckily as far as I know, no one saw any of this. I no longer had the frying pan so I started searching for another weapon that I could use to beat the shit out of David. I picked up a vase from David's bookshelf and went searching. He had locked himself in the bathroom.

"Open this door you bastard. Come on, David, open up," I screamed, while pounding on the door like a wild woman. David didn't budge.

Flashbacks of their lovemaking danced before my eyes. I suddenly felt worn. Pain, hurt enveloped me. I backed up against the wall. The moisture of my mouth had forsaken me. My screaming became mumbling, which turned to incoherent expressions, further blurred by tears. I slid down the wall until I was sitting on the floor crying uncontrollably. I couldn't stop the stinging tears that flooded my eyes and streaked my face. I was completely torn. What I witnessed had finally registered. After all this time, David had betrayed me. My body convulsed and gave way to the pain. David opened the door to the bathroom to see where I was. He just stood gazing at me from around the door. He came out and bent down to hold me. The tighter he held me the more I cried, the more I shuddered. I just let go. I cleansed myself.

"I'm sorry Lexie, Baby, you have to believe me. I love you," David said and lifted my chin to meet his eyes.

With his plea I wiped my tears and stared him directly in his eyes, searching for sincerity in his words. Tears were falling from his eyes as well, and the sincerity was evident.

"Just move away from me," I said.

David sighed and lifted himself. He reached down to assist me to my feet. I relinquished all in my deluge. I had nothing left. No words. I sought understanding through his eyes. I wanted to connect with him spiritually to know that all would be well. My mind and heart decided collectively that it wasn't going to happen. I shook and lowered my head. David lifted my chin and searched my eyes for any inclination that there would be a chance of us getting past this. I slowly removed his hand and turned to walk away. David reached for me then drew his hand back. I walked out without looking back to address him directly.

"I'll be back for my things when I return from L.A."

I quickly dressed and left.

Brian   CHAPTER 4

From my hotel room window there was a scenic view of the sunny City of Angels, with a delicate mix of palm trees and women. I was here on business, but I was sure to engage in a little pleasure as well. I smelled good and looked damn good in my navy blue Brooks Brothers business suit, light blue shirt and Kenneth Cole wing tips. I felt like a freshman at a party chock full of loose and perky college girls.

I had plenty of work to do, but the weather and scenery was working against me. The atmosphere was intoxicating. Women were everywhere. But even so, business was business and all the fun in the world couldn't keep me from making money. I went to my room to freshen up after a lunch meeting with potential clients. A huge financial firm was looking for IT professionals to head up an internet venture the company was launching. I was their top candidate. They wined me, dined me, and tried to convince me that my talents and their company would be the perfect match. I must say, the price was right. They had an opportunity to review the project that I'd just finished, which was on display at my latest client's exhibit booth. The only problem was this firm was headquartered in Chicago. They were trying to influence me to relocate, even though there was a satellite office in New York.

It was a late and long lunch. As far as I was concerned, I was finished for the day. It was time to freshen up and get ready for a night on the town. I wanted to see what L.A. had to offer a man. I planned to meet a fried at a club called The Raven. Women of all walks of life frequented this place. The Raven was a somewhat upscale and popular spot where folks are known to really let their hair down. It wasn't uncommon to catch a celebrity or two inside every now and then. I wanted to experience this place firsthand. Maybe find a honey to keep me company during my visit to this City of Angels. I didn't want a chick falling in love with me in three days and try to follow me back to Brooklyn. I have enough to deal with at home and there is no need to add unnecessary complications to my life.

It was finally time to go. I hopped in my rented Jaguar S-type and perused the streets for a few minutes, trying to check out the sites. I tried to keep within the area that I became familiar with during the day. I was never a punk, but I wasn't trying to get lost in South Central alone. Like I said, I didn't need any more complicated stress in my life. My man, Jeff, was meeting me outside of the club. Jeff is one of my boys from Brooklyn who was representing his company at the conference.

When I pulled up to the club I was definitely impressed. The décor had a little tropical essence to it. I spotted Jeff waiting for me outside near the curb. When he saw me he came up to the car while I parked. Jeff was a tan colored brother with light brown eyes. He stood about six feet. Not a real big guy, but by no means was he small either. Women always flocked to Jeff, however I never saw him take up time with any of the good-looking ones. I wasn't sure if Jeff had bad taste or just didn't want to be bothered with really pretty women. Jeff wore a cream and navy linen shirt; navy linen slacks and blue dress shoes. Jeff greeted me with a pound as I got out the car.

"What's up man? You ready for the ladies or what?" Jeff chuckled and released a wide-mouthed smile.

It was amazing how we brothers are so professional and articulate one minute and as soon as we are amongst ourselves and out of the "professional arena," we turn to, as my father would say, "speakin' easy."

"Yo, what up, what up? What's it like up in there?" I asked Jeff.

"Man, listen. That's all I have to say," he said shaking his head.

I laughed since he really didn't say anything. I knew Jeff. Therefore I knew what he was trying to say.

"That's cool. Let's roll."

I wanted to ask Jeff what cologne he was wearing because it smelled good, but I'm not a sissy so I just admired it in private. I made a mental to remember the scent and go on a smelling spree at the mall and find it for myself.

When we got inside, the club was packed. The atmosphere was nice. The women looked great. Some of them a little underdressed for any occasion but that was okay too.

As soon as we got in, a thick sister spotted Jeff and sashayed her way over towards us. The big smile on her face revealed a space the size of the Grand Canyon between her two front teeth. I looked back to see who she was smiling at until I realized she was coming for us. I started to zero in on the bar area as if I had seen a familiar face. Then I smiled and threw my hand up like I found who I was looking for and headed towards the bar before she could introduce herself. Jeff was left to deal with canyon mouth but didn't seem to mind. I ordered a drink and looked towards the dance floor to see canyon mouth having a ball dancing with an unaffected Jeff. It was clear that Jeff was just out to have fun.

After chilling for a few minutes I spotted this fine sister near the bar with a crazy stressed look on her face. She wore the kind of expression that said, "I have had it up to my eyeballs and the next person that says 'boo' to me is going to get their feelings hurt." I studied her for a moment. She had flair about her even as she wore the look of madness. I thought about it. A man! Only a man can make a women look like that. This sister was sweet. She had a nice brown complexion. Her skin reminded me of a creamy cup of hot cocoa. She had pretty, slightly slanted eyes. Damn! Nice lips; ample breasts, not too big and not too small; and shoulder length jet-black hair hanging down the sides of her well sculpted cheekbones. I couldn't analyze much more because she was sitting, but I could tell that the red suit she wore was nothing cheap. This sister was a classic. I decided to talk to with her, knowing that I had to be careful because I was treading on dangerous ground. I figured I would have some fun with her. I had to think of something to say to Ms. Hot Chocolate.

"So what did he do?" I asked.

For a moment she just stared at me. I was about to retreat because the chick looked at me like she was about to take my head off. Then she snapped out of it.

"I'm sorry, pardon me?" Her voice was soft, calm.

"What did he do to you?" I asked again.

"I'm sorry. Who are you referring to?" She looked confused and annoyed.

I almost left on that note but decided to finish what I started.

"Your man," I smiled, hoping it would make her smile. For

some reason I wanted her to smile.

"My man?" She became indignant.

"Yes, your man," I pressed on.

"What would make you ask me a question like that?"

She held her head back and stared at me though tightly slit eyes.

"The look on your face. Only a man can make a woman wear a look of madness like that."

She laughed. I felt relieved.

"Cute, was that your come on?"

"Actually no, I was really wondering what happened."

"Why that's rather nosy for a stranger," she said.

"I know, but I still want to know," I persisted then flashed what I hoped was a winning smile.

"Well, Mr. Stranger, if you want to know so badly, I caught him in the act."

My dumb ass asked, "The act of what?"

She just looked at me as if she wanted to ask, 'What act do you think I mean?'

"Oh...Oh ...WOW! I'm sorry," I said, finally realizing what she meant.

"So am I," she said and dropped her head.

I was at a loss for words. What was I getting myself into? With all these smiling, sweet looking women in here I would choose to talk with the depressed sister, on the verge of an episode of It's a Thin Line Between Love and Hate. What the hell!

"Would you let me buy you a drink?"

I could have kicked myself for asking. Why didn't I just leave this alone and walk away?

"I don't know," she practically whispered.

"Why don't you know?"

"I already had about six shots of Jack Daniels," she chuckled.

"Wow! Are you going to be all right?"

"I hope so. I guess I will know for sure when I try to walk."

Then she laughed a hearty laugh, probably the first one since she found her man's penis in the other woman.

"Okay. How long have you been here?"

"Since I finished work," She said then sighed and surrendered her thoughts to a pregnant silence. "I'm not trying to be rude, but I'm not looking to get into anything with anyone here. So I don't think you really want to waste your time with me. I'm a little wounded right now." She chuckled then hiccupped.

"Where are you from," I asked, unable to just leave her alone. I felt sorry for her and drawn to her at the same time.

"New York." She looked at me like she wanted to say, "Is this man listening, or what?"

"What part?"

"Why?"

"Because, I'm from Brooklyn. I'm here on business."

I thought again, where am I going with this? All I want was a temporary L.A. honey, no strings attached, to chill with for a couple of days. Why am I not backing off of this sister? She was silent. I wondered what she was thinking, if she was still able to think straight after all that Jack Daniels. I looked around for Jeff who was still dancing with canyon mouth.

"I'm from Brooklyn too."

Her eyes stretched open like a real drunk and she looked like she was about to throw up her stomach lining. Again, I felt for her.

27

I had been there and for some dumb reason I wanted to help her. I felt like she needed a friend.

"Listen, I think you need to get back to your room. You don't look good."

"Gee thanks!" She hiccupped again.

This time I think more than just air came up. She quickly raised her hand to her mouth to catch whatever was threatening to come out. What ever it was, I think she swallowed it.

"Did you drive here?"

"Yes."

She looked as if she was sorry she drove. She sighed again and let her head fall back as she gazed at the ceiling.

"Well how did you plan on getting back to your hotel?"

My father was coming out of me. I realized I was chastising her.

"I never thought about that."

"All right Ms. Got-It-All-Thought-Out."

"Ouch!" She said, scrunched up her nose and then chuckled a little.

"I am going to help you out here, but you gotta trust me. As a matter of fact, you don't have a choice since you are all alone out here. Since you're a fellow Brooklynite, I am going to look out for you. Stay here and give me a minute, I will be right back."

I went to look for Jeff who was now dancing with a long-neck chick that looked like Mr. Ed and let him know I would catch up with him later.

"Man, you work fast," Jeff said.

"I wish." I huffed.

Mr. Charity was back in action. I should just buy a purple cape and place a big C on my chest.

By the time I had gotten back to Ms. Hot Chocolate she had at least made it to her feet.

"I tried to walk and decided I had to trust you, my fellow Brooklynite." Ms. Hot Chocolate proceeded to tell me where she was staying and actually remembered where she had parked.

As soon as I placed her in her rental, she fell asleep. I had to ask directions from some guy on the street to make it to her hotel. There was something sexy about the way she laid curled up in the car in her drunken sleep. She was sleeping hard too. She was about to start drooling when we reached her hotel. Nice place, very nice. I assumed she made a lot of money and had a pretty decent position at her job to be at this place. It was a real ritzy establishment. I realized that I never asked her name when I tried to wake her up to let her know that she was home. The valet guy tapped on my window to ask if I was staying. I told him I could use some help getting her out of the car. He called another guy to help me with Ms. Hot Chocolate and he took her car away. She could barely stand on her feet and practically fell out of the car when we tried to help her out. Finally she woke up tripped up the curb and bumped into an older lady who snarled at her. She turned her lip up at the lady and shot back "ah whatever," then flipped the lady her middle finger. I wanted to laugh my ass off but I managed to maintain my composure.

I finally got Hot Chocolate up to her room, carried her to the bedroom of her one-bedroom business suite, and laid her on the bed. She began snoring immediately. I ordered room service for her and plenty of bottled water. I wasn't sure if she was a vegetarian or not so I order one vegetarian dish and one chicken dish and brewed a pot of coffee. I figured that once I got her to put something in her stomach, drink coffee and a little water, she should be good enough. I knew she was in town on business and didn't want the sister to loose her job to a hangover. We folks must look out for one another.

By the time the food came I managed to get her up with a warm cloth over her face. She looked up at me with distant eyes. I thought to myself, been there done that. I knew what she was feeling.

"Thank you," she said quietly.

"All right Miss, I have to go. I ordered some food, made a pot of coffee, and called for a six o'clock wake up call. I think you will be fine."

"Wait...um...," she said and hesitated.

"Brian," I said, turning back towards her. Even in her sad state she was gorgeous.

She frowned. "Thanks. I appreciate your help."

"You're welcome ...uh."

"Alexia. Everyone calls me Lexie," she said in sweet whisper.

"All right, Lexie, eat up. Don't want you coming all the way to L.A. just to lose your job."

"Thanks again Bri..." She suddenly hoped off the bed covering her mouth to keep the vomit from coming out and headed for the bathroom. I headed for the door.

Lexie   CHAPTER 5

The ringing phone pierced through my dreams. I jumped out of bed so fast I nearly broke my neck. I looked around the room trying to get my bearings straight. Once the room came into focus I noticed my clothing on the floor in a trail leading from the bathroom. Half eaten chicken and vegetables was left on a plate in the bed next to me and a cup of cold, black coffee sat on the nightstand beside me. I noticed that I was in bed naked. I tried to put the pieces together from the night before but only bits and pieces came to me. I couldn't figure out if the pieces were part of last night's events or a dream. The part that appeared to be a dream was the fine brother whose face I couldn't quite recollect. It was ten minutes after six in the morning, and I had a business breakfast to attend at seven. I wanted to get up but was scared I couldn't focus. I tried anyway. All the while I had been holding my head. Afraid to let go because I would feel the pounding that I knew was waiting for me. Slowly I let go and to my surprise the pounding was not there. The pounding came two seconds later but was outside of my head. I thought I was losing my mind. It was the door. "Ms. Mitchell, this is your wake up call. You did not answer your phone."

"I'm awake. Thank you." I yelled back.

I managed to drag myself out of the bed, still putting together pieces of the night before. Things were starting to come into focus. I remember being at the club and then everything skips to my room. Obviously there was a big chunk of time missing. I will have to worry about that later right now I have to get my act together and make this breakfast on time. I turned on the television to the morning news to break the disturbing silence in the room and headed for the shower.

The water was soothing. I found myself standing under the steady stream of water and my mind raced back to yesterday. I saw myself standing at the door of David's home office watching him make love to another woman. I felt my heart break into pieces. I backed up against the wall of the shower sliding down into the tub. I felt like I was floating. The shower water beat down on my back. I let the floodgates open and cried. I cried hard, so hard that my entire body shook. Every emotion known to man worked its way through my being.

I had to compose myself to prepare for my morning meetings. I found solace in the softness of the hotel robe. I oiled my body with some Chanel body oil and attempted to fix my face so that I wouldn't look like a Mack truck hit me. There was another knock at the door. I wondered who it could be, hoping and praying it wasn't my boss Mary Ann. Maybe it's Arthur. Since I got the promotion Arthur has become rather friendly. I guess I wasn't important enough before, but we have actually become pretty good friends. We have had lunch a couple of times and shared some stories about his climb up the corporate ladder. He really is a nice guy and has even become somewhat of a mentor to me.

It was room service with a tremendous spread. I told the server that I hadn't ordered anything, but he advised that someone had ordered for me. I couldn't imagine who would have done that, but I told him to bring it on in and wait while I got him a tip. He told me that everything was already cared for. I peeked into the eloquently displayed platters and there were eggs, bacon, waffles, yogurt, and fruit. Suddenly I was starving, so I sat down and started devouring the food. Halfway through the waffles and eggs, I remembered that I had a breakfast scheduled. I just stuffed myself and had only fifteen minutes to get to my meeting.

The race was on. Within the next fifteen minutes flat I made up my face, did my hair, ironed my brown Ellen Tracy pant suit and threw on a butter-yellow shell and matching Kenneth Cole sandals and flew down to the lobby to meet with the rest of my party. I was so very glad that we agreed to eat here at the hotel. I figured I would just order some coffee and have some fruit. I must admit, after last night's ordeal I was looking rather good. I impressed myself and felt much better.

I hit the lobby with two minutes to spare. No one else was there yet. I found out later that my boss and a few others from the office went out for drinks after the meetings and got wasted. A very familiar man was sitting in the lobby watching me emerge from the elevator. I put a little pep in my step because I knew that I was looking good. Then I recognized the man. He was finer now in his single-breasted, coal gray business suit than he was last night. He was tall and truly handsome. At first I felt a little embarrassed. Then I said to myself, "Oh what the hell. I am not here to impress any one." He stood up and started walking my way. I thought maybe I would want to impress this one a little.

"Good morning Lexie."

"Good morning..." I realized I wasn't quite sure what his

33

name was. I tried hard to recall.

"Brian," he interrupted my memory session with a rich deep voice.

"I was going to say that," I lied and smiled.

"No you weren't," he said with a pretty smile revealing beautiful white teeth and by far the nicest set of lips I had ever seen.

His teeth had to be bleached. I can respect a brother that takes pride in his smile. I was just hoping he didn't lick those lips in front of me. I could feel my loins begin to stir.

"Okay, you got me. Did you order that wonderful spread this morning?" I smiled, unable to tear my eyes away from his lips.

"I had to help my fellow Brooklynite." He smiled too.

"Well, I really appreciated it."

I suddenly felt comfortable with him.

"Yeah well I didn't want to see a sister loose her gig over a man."

"Good looking out. I am very thankful!" I couldn't help smiling.

"Well, I'll see you around. I gotta get to business. I just came over to make sure you were going to be okay," he said.

Though he just said he was going, he didn't move. Neither did I. I continued staring at his lips. He licked them and the walls of my vagina convulsed so strongly I thought he witnessed it.

"Oops," I said out loud and tried to play it off by continuing with the conversation. "I don't know how to thank you. Perhaps I can treat you to dinner later."

He looked at me questionably and raised a single brow. I smiled hard, tying to restrain the laughter clamoring inside.

"Sure, brothers don't turn down food. I'll meet you here. What time?"

"How about eight tonight?" I said with my composure now fully regained.

"That's cool. I gotta get down to business. I'll see you later."

Just like that he was gone. I just stood there for another few minutes with my head in the clouds until my boss' voice snapped me out of it. It was time for business and thanks to my fellow Brooklynite, I was ready, willing and able do my thing. I thought to myself, he is really cool.

The day went well, the morning meetings, the afternoon presentations, and the business dinner. It was now 7:30 and I was a little tired but I didn't want to let Brian down. Besides he had done so much for me that I felt I had to take him to dinner just to show my appreciation. Any other person could have taken full advantage of me. Also since my day was done so early I figured I needed to go out and distract myself instead of sitting in the hotel room crying. Every time I was alone, I cried. Brian was gorgeous anyway. That made him the perfect distraction. I couldn't wait to see his chocolate face, suave goatee and pearly white smile. I could tell he had a chest of iron with strong ripples in just the right places. From the looks of his attire, the brother certainly knew his way around a closet.

I couldn't figure out what to wear. I didn't want to stay in my suit, and I didn't want to make too much of an effort and look overdone. Besides I wasn't very hungry. I had a light dinner with clients knowing I was going to have dinner with Brian afterwards. I pulled my soft yellow, cropped pants out of my bag. Then I got a multi-colored silk halter, soft yellow sandals and small yellow purse. It was just big enough for my wallet, cell phone and shades. The outfit was chic and cute. I knew it would work.

35

It was time to go and I didn't want to keep Brian waiting. He really seemed like a nice guy. He appeared to be one of those cute, nice guys that many women don't take seriously because he lacks adventure and, most of all, drama. Women can be so shallow. Apparently for most women, drama is an attractive characteristic, whether we admit it or not, especially when it comes with good looks. We rather exercise our emotions with gorgeous, troublesome basket cases. I vowed to myself at that moment to be better to myself when it comes to choosing men, and this time I really meant it.

Brian   CHAPTER 6

All through my workout Lexie had been on my mind. I wondered how she was doing these past couple of weeks. I hadn't bothered speaking to her since the conference in L.A. I figured she needed time to handle her situation and I didn't want to be in the middle of that. I don't do rebounds. We did have a good time together starting with dinner the second night and hanging out the other nights acting like tourists, checking out the sites in the City of Angels. We could have done without the ride to Compton. We were both curious to see what they called the ghetto. Being from New York, you always think other places can't be that bad. Damn, was I wrong!

I start my new gig in midtown. The offer was one I couldn't refuse. I was having dinner tonight with Shelly. That chick was really starting to bother me. She was becoming much too possessive and started acting a little crazy. I knew how to spot warning signs, so I figured I needed to bring this 'friendship' to a close. I was looking forward to doing it this weekend. I really needed my space.

It felt good working in Manhattan again. It's been almost a year since I set up a home office and worked only from home for myself. I was due for a change of pace. I loved the fine women swishing up and down Fifth Avenue with attitude, meticulously dressed in their best. My brothers were doing their thing too. I was only a few blocks from Bryant Park, which is filled to the rim with the buppies and yuppies from the surrounding area.

The office building was quite nice. In the lobby of my new office there was a huge mahogany reception area, where a young black receptionist sat on the phone, wearing entirely too much makeup. There was something wrong with her eyebrows, and it made her look like she was asking a question all of the time. Other than that she appeared to be cute. She noticed me the moment I got off of the elevator and stared at me until I reached the reception desk. I said 'good morning.' Without returning a word, she held the phone, slowly stood up to check out my lower half and paused. The she rolled her eyes into the air, sighed, closed her eyes and whispered "Thank you Jesus." She told the person on the phone she had to go and slowly returned her bottom to the chair. I wasn't sure what was going on, so I just stood there.

"Good morning. Can I help you...?" She finally said in a so-called sexy voice.

As I began to respond, Paul Riccardi, one of the guys I met with in L.A., entered the lobby looking for me. Paul was the Director of Business Development and had worked for the company since graduating college. Now in his mid thirties, Paul had a suave look with dark brown hair, a baby face and hazel eyes. Needless to say, Paul was well sought after by his female counterparts.

"Hey Brian, how's it going?"

"Good thanks, Paul." We shook hands.

"Great to see you, come with me." I followed Paul through a pair of floor to ceiling glass doors. Inside there was a large office space filled with gray cubicles surrounded by office doors along the walls. Paul continued as we walked down a long corridor.

"We've got your office and things all set up. I'll introduce you to a couple of folks and uh, give you a chance to get settled. We will have a ten o'clock meeting with the IT staff and lunch with the CTO at one."

"Sounds good to me."

I had a feeling this was a smart move for me.

"I say we get going." Paul offered a cheerful smile.

"Good idea."

"Great having you on board, Brian. I'm sure you'll like it here."

The office was really nice. It had a smooth contemporary look to it. My contract was for six months, but I knew it wouldn't take that long. That's why I agreed on a set fee regardless of the amount of time it took. Once I get them up and running with the new system that I designed for them my work here would be done. From the looks of things, I could really get used to being here.

Paul introduced me to the staff, all who appeared at first sight to be decent folk. Afterwards he led me to the office that I would be using and left me alone. I had an hour and a half before our ten o'clock meeting and basically nothing to do until then. I was still trying to figure out what the deal was with that receptionist.

The day went as well as I had hoped. I met the staff, CTO, and the loony receptionist Shakoyah, who I was warned to stay away from because she was a little weird. I laid out my game plan for their new system and designated projects accordingly. It was now five-fifteen and time to go. I was scheduled to meet Shelly at Virgil's at six. I actually looked forward to seeing her, but braced myself for the unexpected. That's how things had become with her.

Shelly looked especially fine tonight, but I didn't let that trick me. She was still one to watch. Virgil's is normally busy after work. However, we managed to get seated right away. I motioned for Shelly to walk ahead of me, and pulled out a chair for her before taking my own seat.

"So honey how was it, your first day and all? Shelly asked as she shifted in her seat.

"It was cool. The people were friendly. The office was nice. The receptionist was weird." I looked around for our server.

"The receptionist was weird?"

"Yeah, cute, but real weird," I stated indifferently. Shelly's face twisted with agitation. *What did I say this time?*

"Cute? Oh she was weird but cute, huh." Shelly curled her lip and rolled her eyes.

I didn't know where this was coming from, so I just sat back and waited for whatever was coming next. Shelly looked as if she wanted to cry and then her weird little frown turned into a sick-looking smile. Then she got started.

"Brian, honey where do you see us going?" She asked as if she fell into a brand-new mood.

"What do you mean?"

I played stupid, as men are instructed to do whenever this question is raised.

"You know what I mean," she whined.

"No I don't know what you mean," I said, keeping the stupid act going.

She blew out air and stared at me. "Brian, we have been seeing each other for a while now you know, and I just wanted to... you know... have an understanding of whether or not this is going to go any further."

"Why? Where do you want this to go?"

"Oh come on, Brian. You know how I feel about you." Shelly stated in her usual pouting tone.

"Shell, can we just let things happen and go with the flow. I'm not ready for anything serious."

Shelly straightened her posture.

"Fine, I'll hang out for a little while, but not too long. Besides I don't see other people," she said.

"Okay." I didn't even acknowledge that last part because I didn't want to go there with her. She had to know I knew that was a flat out lie.

After dinner we went back to my place for a little desert. Shelly stopped talking her stuff for a little while but soon went right back to it. So I played tired, hoping that would annoy her and keep her from staying all night. Apparently she had plans of her own. So when I realized she wasn't going anywhere, I threw on some music and went to take a shower and get ready for bed.

The shower felt really good. Suddenly I felt a knot in the pit of my stomach. That's my body's way of letting me know that something isn't right. So I jumped out of the shower, wrapped my towel around my waist and headed for my bedroom. When I walked into the room, Shelly was bent over near my dresser writing something. I startled her and she nearly jumped out of her skin.

"Shelly, what are you doing?"

"N...nothing. Why?" She stuttered and tried to hide the item she was writing on.

"What are you writing?"

Then out of nowhere she went from startled to irate.

"What do you mean what am I writing? Do you want to tell me

who Alexia Mitchell is?" she scowled.

"Why?" I could see the crap stew brewing.

"Why? What do you mean, 'why'?"

She grabbed her chest. I could tell she was about to begin one of her award-winning performances.

"Shelly, why would I want to tell you who Alexia Mitchell is? I don't see how that concerns you."

This entire act was now very old to me. Shelly was filled with rage.

"How dare you say that to me? After all I've done for you!"

I was getting pissed. I was tired, cold, and not in the mood for this crazy mess. So I snapped right back at her.

"What the hell do you mean after all you've done for me? Where is all of this coming from?" I threw my hand in the air.

"Brian, you know if it weren't for me, you wouldn't even live here."

Shelly's father owned a lot of real estate. He put in a good word for me when I wanted to buy this condo. So I skipped having to go through all the red tape to get in.

"Shelly, please, that was three years ago and you act as if you paid for the place for me. Don't act like I couldn't have gotten this place or any other place like this on my own. What is really wrong with you?"

"What is WRONG with me? It's not me, it's you!" she screamed.

Here we go again. First of all, I didn't know how we got here or why. Shelly looked like she was in a fight. Her hair was loosening from the roll she had it in, and her mascara was running down her face from her tears. I didn't understand the need for the tears. This had to end now.

"Listen, Shelly, I don't know what the deal is with you, but I don't have time for this. I think it's time for you to leave."

"Just like that, huh."

Shelly threw her hands in the air for emphasis. She was fuming.

"Yeah just like that." I said indifferently.

I ignored her and continued about my business. I walked over to the dresser to get clean boxers to sleep in. When she saw me heading in the direction of the dresser she shot across the room to beat me there. I thought she had lost her mind. Not knowing what to expect, I braced myself for an impact. Then I noticed my phone book open on the dresser. I had left Lexie's card in my book and never took the time to write her number into the book. Shelly launched at me before I could pick up the phone book and attempted to grab it. I snatched it off of the dresser before she could get to it. She actually fought me for my phone book, screaming the entire time. I held the book in my hand above my head as Shelly jumped up and down trying to snatch it from my hand. I had to laugh. What was wrong with this chick?

She became so enraged after I laughed that her face paled with anger. I stopped laughing long enough to sit her down on my bed to calm her down. She fruitlessly tried to escape my grasp. Despite my grip, she continued to try and take hold of the book. I became mad all over again.

"Shelly what is wrong with you?" I shouted.

She truly challenged my level of tolerance.

Shelly was captured by the sharpness of my tone.

"Don't shout at me," she wined and began crying.

Shelly fell apart, covering her face with her hands.

"Shelly…"

I was spent. I just wanted to know what all of this was really about. I dropped my hand to my side and sighed.

Shelly dropped her head and hands and turned away. She then caught site of Lexie's card on the floor and lunged for it. In one fell swoop, she scooped the card and tried to rip it to pieces. I snatched it from her just in time.

"You know what? It's time for you to leave."

I grabbed Shelly by the arm to lead her out of the bedroom. She jerked her arm from my grasp.

"Oh, so now you're gonna just kick me out?"

Shelly was ranting and shaking her head like a mad child who was just told she couldn't go to her best friend's birthday party. I couldn't believe this. I halted and raised both hands to my temples.

"You know what?" I mumbled through clenched teeth.

My finger found its way to claim opposition a mere hair's length from her nose. Before I could say anything else, Shelly ran out the bedroom.

Now further incensed, I turned and noticed something very bizarre about my phone book. Shelly had transposed several of the telephone numbers. She changed threes to eights, sevens to nines and ones to sevens. When I looked for her number she had written "wifey" next to it. Luckily she didn't have a chance to destroy Lexie's card. I felt heat surge within me. I heard Shelly rummaging through the living room and assumed she was gathering her belongings to leave. Somewhat relieved, I charged into the living room after her, still in nothing more than my bath towel that was losing its grip. Just as I reached the entrance to the living room, Shelly had her coat, her purse and a large green garbage bag by the door. My energy was depleted.

"What's in the bag Shelly?" I asked. I knew Shelly hadn't left any clothes or any other belongings for that matter, therefore whatever was in the bag had to belong to me. I was just uncertain about what the contents of that bag could be.

"Screw you Brian!" she yelled and glared at me through slit eyes.

My hands went to my hips as I nodded in disbelief. I didn't know she was this crazy. I reached for the bag. Shelly charged and attempted to snatch the bag from me. My towel unraveled and fell to the floor gracefully, in contrast to the tumultuous scene. The bag had torn, offering a glance at my captive couch pillows. I could only give her a bewildered stare. She really and truly lost her mind. I was oblivious to my own nakedness before her. Shelly's head plunged in shock. She froze, wide-eyed with her mouth agape.

"Why are you taking my couch pillows?" She didn't respond.

"SHELLY!" I shouted.

Shelly lowered her eyes. Her gaping mouth closed. Her shoulders slumped. With closed eyes, she raised her head and released a sigh satiated with defeat.

"It was supposed to be all about you and me, Brian. Okay? Why couldn't it just be all about you and me? Why can't you love me the way I love you?"

Shelly dropped her arms heavily to her side as her shoulders shook from the onset of tears.

My eyes rolled into my head trying not to believe what I witnessed. I no longer felt the desire to play a supporting role in Shelly's recitation. Not once have I ever misled her, even as it became obvious that she wanted more from me than I wanted from her. It was time to bring closure to this indeterminate association.

"Look, Shelly, it's time for you to leave. I'm done and this is over," I said trying to control my tone.

Without another word, Shelly retrieved her bag and coat and quietly headed for the door.

"I bought you those pillows, I want them back!" she shouted and stormed out slamming the door behind her.

I sent Shelly the pillows the next day by Fed Ex. Who needed couch pillows anyway?

Lexie   CHAPTER 7

There was a knock at the door. I wasn't expecting anyone, so I was willing to let the person continue knocking. I thought about the situation with David all night long and wondered how to handle the whole thing. I couldn't absorb the entire ordeal and attempted to deal with it in small doses. I pondered how one aspect of my life was going so well while the other was going down the drain. A few times I had thought about Brian back in L.A. and wanted to call him, but I knew I didn't need to speak to him.

The person at my door continued knocking. Grudgingly I removed myself from the couch to answer. A fairly young, but cute delivery guy asked me to sign for a package. I dragged the huge box in the house, wondering what it was. I hadn't ordered anything lately. The handwriting on the air bill resembled David's. Using a kitchen knife I opened the box to find all my belongings that were left at David's house. That bastard! An envelope greeted me atop the contents of the box. I ripped oven the envelope to find more of the handwriting that resembled David's:

I'm sorry. I figured this would be the best way. D.

The floodgates opened again.

For the next few weeks I put every ounce of my time and energy into work and working out. Pain and embarrassment held me from disclosing the details of our break up with anyone. Eventually I cried less and less until there were no more tears. I often thought about Brian, but didn't want to be the first to call. I eventually became displeased with him as well because he hadn't called me by now. He knew how to reach me. We swapped work, home, and cell phone numbers as well as our home and work e-mail addresses. He could have run a credit check on me had I given him any more of my personal information. I wondered what he thought about me due to the circumstance under which we met. Refusing to be the first to call, I let go of him too.

Brooke talked me into going out on a date with an old friend of mine who works with her. Ronald Covington was kind and good-looking. He had fair, tan skin, and long luscious eyelashes. Alas he was materialistic, butchered the English language and tried entirely too hard to be cool, which annoyed the hell out of me. We attempted dating in the past, but I couldn't stand too much of him. I stopped calling, and he faded away. Then he began working with Brooke and would ask about me constantly until Brooke finally enlightened him about my break up with David. I decided what the hell? I had nothing better to do.

Ronald picked me up around seven-thirty in the evening. When I entered the car he wore an ungainly smile as his gaze washed across my body. His eyes sauntered from my breast to graze over the interior of his car. He smiled back at me, self-assured of my approval of his luxury vehicle. I intentionally alleged nothing. After a few seconds he smiled, rolled his eyes up in his head and started to pull off. I prepared myself mentally for whatever the rest of the evening would bring.

"So wuzz up baby, it's been a long time," he said.

"Yes, it has been a long time. How have you been?"

"You know me, boo. I'm all right," he said and smiled.

I could see all thirty-two teeth.

"So where are we headed tonight?" I asked, thinking, "how soon will this be over?"

"Yeah, I got something real nice in store for 'ta night. You could use that, right?"

His gaiety was beginning to irk me and the night had only begun. I wanted to tell him to turn the car around and take me home. I decided against it for the sake of courtesy to Ron. And, at the very least, I deserved to try and enjoy myself. I began to humor myself by making a special effort to note all of his wretched attempts at speaking good ol' English. By the end of the night I had counted numerous mispronounced words–five that he had to have made up on his own and four big words that were sorely misused. I think one of my all time favorites was "artinerary," misused for "itinerary." The other was when he said that he thought that I was very "observative" instead of observant. I exploded into an endless fit of mirth. The more I drank, the funnier he became. Eventually I truly began to enjoy his company, or maybe it was just the apple martinis.

We had dinner at a trendy Vietnamese restaurant in the Village. The food was great. After dinner we went to a nearby cabaret for more drinks and a little dancing. Ron has always been a great dancer. By the time we left the bar, I was charged. Even his bad English made sense to me. After a pretty decent evening, we went back to his place. The mood was right and I was in need of a little maintenance.

My nipples hardened, making it hard for me to conceal my erotic desires. Ronald stood before me, removing his attire piece by piece. The more he removed the higher my desire rose. Ron slowly slid his boxers down his firm muscular legs. He bent to remove them from entrapping his ankles. A pungent odor wafted throughout our surroundings, taking my nostrils hostage. I searched for the source of the ghastly aroma when I detected the mucky train traveling along the center of his entangled boxers. The odor emanated from his boxers. There was no way I was going to let this man screw me with his behind smelling the way it did. I devised a plan for an escape. A scream escaped my lips before I realized it had surfaced from my own mouth. So I just went along with the program.

"What's wrong baby?"

Ron was startled and became alarmed.

"My stomach! Oh my God! Aaaaahhh!"

I doubled over and Ron reached for me, giving rise to his stinking behind. I couldn't fathom how he was completely oblivious to the stench that radiated from his backside.

"What's the matter, baby what's hurting you?"

He appeared to be so concerned.

"Oh my God my stomach, a... ahh... sharp pains. It must have been something I ate." I gasped.

Ron bent over to tend to me and that smell shrouded the atmosphere. Still screaming, I slid to the floor and panted.

"No–don't worry. This is not the first time. I've got to go." Scrambling for my scattered undergarments and dress, I haphazardly clothed myself and raced for the door. Ron ran after me. I shot outside before he could reach me realizing he was still naked and would not likely follow me out the door.

"You don't have your car remember? Let me take you to the hospital or something," he said calling after me.

"NO! I mean...that's okay. Please, don't trouble yourself. Don't worry. I'll call you."

I trotted to the nearest car service and headed home in the first thing smoking. I haven't seen or heard from Ron "Stinky-Man" Covington, since then.

The constantly ringing phone had taken residence in my apartment. I became used to letting the phone ring because I was tired of answering questions like, "How are you doing?" and "Are you all right?" I didn't want to hear Brooke's harsh words of wisdom nor Dionne and Ava's pity-laced conversations. I surely didn't want to hear from "Mr. Stinky Man." I couldn't take the nagging ringing so I snatched the phone off of the receiver and snapped an obviously irritated "hello" into the receiver.

A befuddled "hello" replied back.

For a minute I thought it was David. I was tired of hanging up on him, so I just stood there with the phone to my ear without responding.

"Hello," the deep voice stated once more.

This definitely wasn't David. If not David, then who?

"May I speak to Alexia Mitchell?"

The rich voice sounded familiar. It came to me. Brian.

"Alexia speaking," I said in a much calmer tone. I tried to sound sexy.

"Did I call at a bad time?"

"No," I said a little too fast.

"Are you all right?" He crooned with his sweet, sexy voice. My shoulders relaxed and tension seeped from my body.

"Yes, I'm fine. So how are you, stranger?" I said loosing a little of my composure.

His voice was like hot caramel being poured over an ice cream sundae.

"Oh, you know my voice," he said with a smile in his tone.

"Yes, I don't know how. I haven't spoken to you in almost two months. And, I don't think I've spoken to you on the phone before," I tried to recall.

"Yes you have," he sung.

"Oh really, when?"

"In Los Angeles."

"Oh, you're right. You've got me" I blushed, setting my cheek-bones on fire.

Brian and I ended up talking on the phone over two hours. We filled each other in on everything, including all the drama that we had been through over the past few weeks. He told me about some crazy, stalker chick named Shelly and how she changed his ladies' numbers in his phone book. I laughed so hard I thought my side was going to split. He told me how she tried to apologize, asked him to marry her and threw a fit when he reminded her that they weren't even together. I told him about my rendezvous with Mr. Stinky-Man and all about David sending my things the day after I got home and how he still calls me to explain even though he was still dealing with the woman. I also told him that I found out that she is an unemployed thirty-year-old, wanna-be rapper with two children named Diamond and Alize.

We arranged an evening out for the upcoming Friday night. We decided not to make definite plans and agreed to play the evening by ear. The conversation was the most fun I had had since returning from LA. I was refreshed and thankful.

Brian   CHAPTER 8

Lexie appeared to have gotten past her episode with her ex-boyfriend. However one must always tread carefully when dealing with a woman scorned. Indeed–dangerous territory. I anticipate she'll have difficulty trusting men initially. I wasn't interested in paying her ex boyfriend's debt. I believed I would really like her but still needed to feel her out first. I flashed back to Shelly, shuddered, and attempted to shake her from my thoughts. I wished her well and thanked the Lord that I found out about her mental state before it was far too late.

53

My night out with Lexie was great. We ate at a quaint café in downtown Brooklyn, took a walk in Prospect Park, and talked about everything under the sun. We discussed where we both were mentally, emotionally and physically. We discussed career and personal goals. We talked about favorite foods, likes and dislikes. We ended up in my condo having cocktails and watching old Dolomite movies. We called it a night when the fuzz from the TV stole into sweet dreams of one another as we lay across the floor and couch. Lexie gathered her belongings, said she had a great night, let me know that she would call me and implored me to stay cool. It turned out we didn't live very far from each other. A short drive, but not exactly walking-distance.

Over the next couple of weeks, Lexie and I became very close. She had become a sounding board for me when I needed to discuss the job and family, or overcome the demonic women of my past. She called on me when she needed to release stress or just to talk. We worked out together, hung out together, played laser tag at the big arcade on Forty-Second Street and cooked for one another. She offered her insight on my female counterparts and I returned the favor. Sex had yet to enter into the picture, but the tension was certainly ever-present. We built a friendship and neither one of us wanted to rock the boat. Ultimately it was my intention to construct a foundation that could withstand the turbulence that would inevitably shroud our lives once we elevated our relationship to higher ground. I wanted more and was determined to get it right this time.

We kissed a couple of times, but that was it. We kept our parts tuned up by those we kept on the side. Even my boys got to know her well and wondered why I never tried to 'get any.' They all thought she was a cool person, but too fine to be considered 'just a friend.'

As much as I confided in Lexie, there was one thing I didn't tell her about–my trip. Actually I didn't know how to tell her. I was afraid of what the time away would do to our friendship and the prospect of a real relationship. I had arranged to take a couple of months for an expedition, a dream trip that I had always marveled at the concept of experiencing. I planned a three-month spree in Europe. I was at a point in my life where I could finally pursue my dream. My only trepidation was leaving Lexie behind. She had obliviously gotten the best of me. Even my buddy Lori advised,

"Don't let this one go."

I needed to figure out a way to make sure she would be around when I returned. I had one month to go before taking off. There was no time to waste. I had to tell her about my trip right away.

The phone rang and stole me from my thoughts. It was Jeff.

"Yo, man you gotta come down here and talk to this girl!" Jeff huffed in an exasperated tone.

I had no idea what he was talking about.

"What's up man? What girl?"

"Shelly!"

My head cocked in confusion. Shelly? What was Jeff talking about? What was she up to now? Shelly was the last person I expected. Then again, she was always full of surprises and Shelly knew how to use Jeff. Just when I assumed this was over, there she was with some brand new drama. This chick was obsessed. I had succeeded at nothing to rid my life of this woman. She once tried to start some mess with Lexie but quickly realized she was out of her league. She recalled Lexie's name from the incident in my room and would constantly ask annoying questions about her. I braced myself for what was to come.

"She is tripping man," Jeff said. I could tell just how aggravated he was from his tone.

"I don't have time for this. Damn, what's it gonna take?" I was pissed now.

"I don't know man but she won't leave unless I get you to come and talk to her. You've got to get this crazy chick from in front of my door," Jeff pleaded.

"All right, I'll be right there," I said and hung up the phone. I just stood for a minute trying to collect my thoughts. I decided this would undoubtedly be the last time I would deal with this chick. What caused her to resurface this time? I thought about calling Lori to come down to Jeff's house with me and then thought better of that idea. Lori wasn't exactly fond of Shelly and would be likely to offer her a good thrashing. It was best that I handled this on my own.

When I turned the corner to Jeff's house, I could see Shelly standing outside of his four-story walk up. As soon as she saw my car turn the corner, she leaped into her car and drove off before I could reach the front of Jeff's house. Jeff came out laughing.

"Damn man, what did you do to that girl?" Jeff said stammering through his amusement.

"I don't know, man," I shook my head.

"What makes that woman act like that? No disrespect but that's one crazy bitch! She did all of that carrying on and the moment you turn the corner she runs off like she saw the devil himself," Jeff joked.

"She's just sick. She started that crazy business when we got back from L.A. She even tried to take my couch pillows."

Jeff fell out laughing. I had to laugh too, just thinking back to the scene.

"What did she want with your couch pillows?" Jeff said, taking a seat on his front stoop.

"She said she bought them and because we weren't dealing, she wanted them back."

"You can't be serious," Jeff threw his head back in awe, clearly amused.

"No lie."

I shook my head and placed my hand in the pockets of my

sweats. I didn't want Jeff to see my hands shaking. I had too much to deal with right now. I appreciated his making light of the situation; I just didn't take this scene lightly. Inside I was furious.

I joined Jeff on his steps, and we kicked it for about another hour. I filled him in on some of the other drama Shelly was dishing, like the time she tried to claim she was pregnant when she found out Lexie and I had been seeing each other on a regular basis. I also told him about how she spied on me and Lexie one night. She followed us to Lexie's house and called me on my cell phone to let me know that she was outside and that I better come out immediately or I would have no car windows. When she saw Lexie come out with a frying pan in her hand instead of me, she drove off. Then I filled him in on the situation with Lexie and my upcoming trip. Jeff warned me to stop playing with that girl and do what I had to do. The fact was I had no intention of playing games with Lexie. We chewed the fat for another half-hour before Jeff left me with his insight.

"Whatever you did to Shelly, don't do it to Lexie or you'll have two crazy bitches on your hand."

I laughed and took my tired self home, went to sleep and dreamed about Lexie.

Lexie   CHAPTER 9

Life started to settle down. I became the old Lexie again. I was back to being my old zany self. I looked and felt damn good after spending so much time in the gym. I lost about 15 pounds and gained definition—just in time for the nice weather.

Things heated up with Brian. I cared about him and had a pretty good idea that he felt the same for me. We established a flirty but close friendship with little intimacy. God knows I wanted more but I held my ground. I had been hurt to badly in the past and didn't want to make hasty mistakes. Also, he had drama in his life with Shelly. I couldn't picture having to deal with the entire scene as a girlfriend.

I was content. I knew that one day Brian would be mine for good. The hard part was playing... I mean being just his friend. Brian, he was a keeper.

Brooke called to see what I was doing for the evening. It was a beautiful, spring Friday. I hadn't been out with the girls in ages. I searched my closet for a funky get-out-and-get-busy outfit to don for the evening. I decided on an iridescent pantsuit, the color reminiscent of a full-bodied glass of merlot. The halter-top was decorated with delicate beading matching the hemline of the capri pants. I added sandals to show off my freshly painted toes. I released the large pins guarding my recently wrapped hair. Pleased by my mirrored reflection, I was transformed and ready for a superb girl's night out.

Brooke pulled up around eight. We wanted to get an early start and begin the evening with a nice dinner. We headed uptown to a quaint bar and lounge called Perks. Frankly, Perks wasn't as quaint as it was tight, however you were guaranteed a great time and succulent shrimp. The atmosphere was lively and the food tasted absolutely divine. I tried my best to eat my shrimp like a lady, but they were so delicious I appeared more like a hungry cow grazing in a pasture. I had lost all control and didn't even care. Dionne intended to meet us there but told us to start without her because she was likely not to eat. We devoured our meals and had to sit for a good twenty minutes just to let the food settle. We couldn't chance having pouting abdomens ruin the looks we had so diligently created.

Brooke looked simply gorgeous. She donned a pair of jazzy, red leather pants along with a beige leather halter that angled across her ample hips. She sported a pair of beautiful beige sandals by Via Spiga with crystal embossed straps the lay gingerly across her own freshly painted toes. Her petite Christian Dior handbag matched her shoes exactly. I had to give it to her, she looked like a million bucks—or at least as if she'd spent a million on her outfit. Brooke kept her naturally long hair, closely cropped. Once she got old enough to cut it, she refused to ever let it grow long again. Brooke was effortlessly stunning and consistently turned heads of men and women alike. Tonight was no exception.

Dionne finally joined us looking as cute as ever. We were having a wonderful time when some guy floated across the room donning a sparkling tight black shirt that could have passed for the image of the Milky Way. That was 'no-no' number one. Then he flashed a winning smile and proudly displayed his hardware, diamond-encrusted, platinum teeth with what appeared to be his initials engraved in the center. I knew right then he was coming for me. I asked out loud "Why me." As soon as I said it, both Dionne and Brooke spotted him and smiled.

"You get them every time," Brooke said. "Just get ready." She teased sipping her signature rum and coke.

"'Scuse me miss, how you doin' tonight?"

My first thought was 'first of all I thought the word excuse me started with an "E?"

"Fine," I whispered and took a sip of my white zinfandel. I tried my best to look uninterested but he wasn't giving up. As I looked closer, the picture further degenerated. He put his hand up on the bar near me revealing an obnoxious display of tawdry jewelry. He had two huge "platinum and ice" rings on each hand, a massive silvery diamond bracelet on one wrist that looked like he had escaped from a chain gang somewhere and a gold nugget watch on the other. That's when I knew I had to get out of there. I began thinking of how to escape as he closed in on me.

"I was watchin' you from 'cross the room. You sure looking all right tonight!"

I watched as shots of saliva leapt from his lips spraying the vicinity. I leaned back as he continued. He must have escaped from the eighties with all those jewels, save the year two thousand twist incorporating the platinum, white gold, silver—whatever it was. He represented at least three decades. When he spoke spit flew from his decorated mouth. I felt like I could use a good shower.

I said in a faux British accent, "I am so sorry darling, but I am about to be on my way. I think I have taken in enough for the night. Do have a good time."

Brooke and Dionne tried their best to maintain their composure. Their smiles fought to stand behind their facial facades.

Mr. Player said, "Ooh an' she got an accent."

His lisp spawned shower mists into the atmosphere again. Suddenly silence overtook his unrelenting spiel as I zeroed in on a rather large round of saliva fleeing his lips, taking aim at my eye. Unable to move, I witnessed the impending assault. I flinched a mere millisecond before the spit made contact, landing just below my right eye. On contact, disgust generated tremors that shook my body while the spit initiated a tingling sensation, setting fire to my cheek. I carefully turned and slammed my wine glass atop the counter. I redirected my attention to my assailant, raised my hands in protest, sighed, and marched off to the cramped ladies room. I left snagga-tooth right where he stood. Brooke and Dionne followed suit with tears of laughter stinging their eyes. Within the solace of the ladies room, we each lost our composure. We laughed until tears stained our faces and the muscles of our abdomens constricted.

"Why me?" I whined.

Brooke was doubled over grasping her constricted flat abdomen. "What is it about you? You get them every time, I swear it never fails!"

"Isn't it the truth? Look at me. What am I, a freak magnet?" I shrugged my shoulders and held my hands in surrender to the concept.

"Girl you ought to be mad. I wouldn't blame you," Brooke

said and laughed again.

Dionne said. "I had enough when I saw the gold nugget watch. When I saw the shiny shirt I said to myself, 'this man is...'"

"Dead wrong," we said together. Our quip for when someone does or wears something they have no business doing or wearing.

"At least we can tell people we know what MC Hammer is up to these days."

We all fell out and laughed until we practically wet our pants.

After refreshing our faces, it was time to move on with the night. We were having a great time and weren't ready to go home. We decided to hit another popular lounge called Jimmy's Uptown Café. I looked forward to going to this place because I hadn't been there before, but I heard plenty about it. As we were leaving Perks, a group of guys were making their way in. Each one was fine as hell and dapper from head to toe. They politely stepped out of the door to let us out and the staring match began. Each one of them eyed us up and down from head to toe and we of course returned the favor. These guys were clean cut with no bulky jewelry and nice clothes. One had a single diamond in his ear that just topped off his entire package. We watched, waiting to exhale.

"Leaving so soon?" Mr. Diamond ear asked.

His voice was smooth. Extremely smooth. Instead of responding us three buffoons just looked at each other.

"Yes we are, and I wish you had come a little earlier," Brooke, the outspoken one said.

They let the door go and started chatting with us. They wanted to know where we were going next. Dionne let the cat out of the bag before anyone could speak. She had her eye on the dark one. He was the essence of tall dark and handsome. He almost looked like Michael Jordan.

"Well do you mind if we hang with you tonight?" Mr. Diamond asked.

Brooke and her big mouth said, "Not at all, let's roll."

Never let it be said the Brooke allowed her bashfulness to restrain her. You can tell these men were not the ones you take home to mama. From what I gathered they were hardly the type that stuck around for more that a few dates. We all know the type. Mr. Diamond's name was Dante. I thought that was fitting. Tall, dark and hansome's name was Caz, short for I don't know what. And last but not least, the last one who was the cutest of them all was Don. I thought that was fitting also. I'm sure he did too.

After a few minutes of chatting, the guys went to get their car, an Escalade. I expected as much. Don was driving. We jumped in our car and set out to conquer Jimmy's Café. The ride to Jimmy's was fun and full of excitement. The three of us were like little girls again. The guys rode next to us all the way and kept the conversation going from light to light. We ended up going to Jimmy's and hanging with these guys for the rest of the night and going to a diner for and early breakfast at about four in the morning. None of us had any intention of taking this chance meeting any further, especially Dionne whose man was at home.

Nonetheless, we certainly had a great time. The guys paid for all of our drinks as well as breakfast. They showered us with expensive bottles of champagne throughout the night. The time came for our meeting in the ladies' room, where we discussed the fact that although the guys were gorgeous and refused to let us pay for our drinks and meals that we hoped they didn't think any of us were going home with any of them. We freshened ourselves up and headed back to the table. It was time to go home. I was as tired as I could possibly be, and I knew that after all that wine I would be no good to anyone tomorrow. Accomplishments – none! Not for the next twelve to twenty-four hours.

We ended up not having to ward off the brothers. Mr. Diamond, Dante, and I exchanged numbers. Don and Brooke did the same. Dionne explained to Caz that she had a man. Caz offered his number just in case the future led her his way. Dionne politely declined. Caz shrugged and respectfully resigned his offer.

I had almost forgotten what it was like to hang out and meet men. I must say it was a good night.

I was sure Dante was going to be trouble and assumed that this "friendship" would surely be short lived. I decided to just have fun while it lasted.

Brian   Chapter 10

Shelly must have moved on with her life unless she decided to take a break. A week had passed and I heard nothing of her. I was happy as hell. I sat pondering in the dark. Thoughts of Lexie occupied my mind. My trip was drawing near and I couldn't decide the best way to address my upcoming departure. Lexie was everything I wanted in a woman. What turned me on the most was that she possessed an air of confidence and appeared oblivious of her own beauty. Hanging with her was like hanging with the boys, except I could picture myself making love to Lexie.

The ringing of the telephone interjected my thoughts. I looked at the time—eleven p.m. It wasn't normal for me to get late calls on weekdays. I realized how tired I was. I was hesitant to answer and decided to retire after taking the call.

"Yo!" I answered informally.

"Hey, what's up partner?" Lexie's soft sweet voice floated through the phone. The "hey" lingered a moment. The muscles in my groin responded.

"What's up you? Isn't it past your bedtime?" I quizzed.

"Don't you know it? I can't sleep, so I decided to call you. Did I wake you?" Her voice was soft and apologetic.

"No. I was up," I said.

"Are you sure? Why?" Lexie asked softly.

Her voice was getting to me, comforting me with its suppleness.

"I've got a lot on my mind."

"Wanna talk?"

"It's nothing big."

"Okay, I am so tired but I just can't sleep. I hope I'm not disturbing you."

"No it's cool. I told you I was up too."

Lexie's voice was sultry, deepened by sleeplessness. She sounded sexy as hell to me. My penis pulsated this time.

"Brian?" she crooned softly.

"Yeah."

"… Never mind." She was holding back.

"Are you okay, Lexie?"

"Yeah, just a lot on my mind. I didn't mean to bother you. I should let you go to sleep. Doesn't make any sense keeping you up too. I'll catch up with you tomorrow. All right partner?"

"Cool," I was reluctant to let her go.

Silence. We held on.

"…Later baby," Lexie said before she hung up.

I held the phone for moments after. I closed my eyes and imagined Lexie before me naked. My penis throbbed. I eased my hand inside of my boxers to massage the growing muscle. I fell into the rhythm of the music playing in the distance and stroked my erect penis to a soothing climax. I massaged my man until I could no longer stand my own touch. All of the muscles in my body began to spasm. My body shook and my juices flowed like lava seeping from a volcano. I relaxed and thanked Lexie.

I shook it off and found myself back at square one at home

alone thinking about Lexie. What was I to do about her? Then I did what women do. I analyzed tonight's brief encounter, remembering that she called me "baby" before she hung up. A healthy smile stole its way across my lips. I had to tell her about my trip. I decided right then that there was no time better than the present. I ran to the bathroom and freshened up. I pulled out a new pair of boxers. It doesn't matter how good a brother is living, underwear is always an afterthought until a woman comes to mind. I slid on sweats and a T-shirt, spayed a hint of D&G cologne and headed over to Lexie's place.

Lexie's lights were on. I assumed she was still up because it had been less than an hour since we'd spoken. I banked on her having trouble sleeping. At first I hesitated. What the hell am I doing over here? I decided to just go through with it and knocked on Lexie's door.

"Who is it?" Lexie sounded annoyed.

Damn! "Lexie, it's me Brian."

"Oh," her voice was calm. "Just a minute," she said.

After what seemed like forever, she finally opened the door to let me in.

"What's up, partner? she yawned. "What brings you over at this time of the night?" Lexie slanted her neck to take note of the time from her wall clock. It was after midnight. Lexie wore a soft-yellow, full-length silk robe with only panties underneath. No bra at all! You had to be looking pretty hard to tell. I imagined she slept naked and went to her room to get the panties and the robe before allowing me in. The silhouette of her plump round breast robbed me of my concentration. Heat invaded my personal space. I started looking around her place as if I had never been there before to distract myself.

"What makes you call a brother at this time of night? I asked.

"I'm sorry, B. I didn't mean to disturb you. I had been think-ing and needed to talk. So I just called you. I dialed your number before I knew it. You're not mad are you?" she playfully pouted.

Lexie motioned for me to have a seat on her leather couch, and then sat on the opposite end with one leg bent under her but-tocks facing me.

"No, I'm not mad."

Now back to my original question. What's up with the after-hours visit?"

I shrugged my shoulders and said, "Couldn't sleep."

We both laughed because we knew that was only half true. She watched me watch her lips. My gaze washed over her settling on the soft outline of her ripe breast. I witnessed her nipples slightly hard-en. The temperature rose despite the fact that it was only spring.

Lexie offered me something to drink and told me to relax while she went to get it. I watched her ass sway as she glided off to the kitchen, appearing to float like she was in a scene from one of Spike Lee's movies. I was hypnotized. My manhood lifted from its slum-bered state attempting to see what all of the commotion was about. I had to focus on something else because wearing sweats were always a dead give away. I shifted in my seat and thought about Shelly. It worked. A single thought about Shelly did the trick. Lexie returned with two tall glasses of cranberry juice. My man's slumber was not going to last. Lexie handed me the glass of juice and sat her fine ass next to me on her tan leather couch and aimed the remote at the TV. Something was on but I don't think either of us paid any attention. We sat enjoying comfortable silence for at least fifteen minutes.

"So what's up Brian?" Lexie asked.

"You." I said and stood.

I reached over to Lexie. She took my hand and stood with me. I cupped her soft face in my hands and pulled her to me, kissing her long, firm, and deliberately releasing all the passion I harbored. The kiss stole her breath. Lexie held her hand at to the nape of my neck and pulled me in. The heat in the room rose higher. For once I wanted to take things nice and slow. My desire for Lexie led the way. I caressed every inch of Lexie's body that I could access while I kissed her. I caressed her shoulders, back, hair, arms, behind and breast with a special gentleness reserved for only her. Her soft lips parted slightly when I reached her most prized possession. I slid my finger between her legs and felt her through her lace underwear. Her body slightly convulsed. I cupped her firm round bottom, massaged her cheeks and pulled her closer to me so that she could feel the effect of my passion for her. I fingered the area around her nipples, sliding my hands inside her robe. I slowly removed the silky garment to the end of her shoulders. It gracefully fell away from her waiting body. Her breast stood firm, beckoning me. Her nipples revealed her own desires. Her body was warm. Lexie allowed me to take the lead. I took her breast into my hand and massaged them while I studied her from head to toe, drinking in all of her beauty from her full, pouting lips, to her perfect toes, and back to her desire-filled eyes.

I lifted Lexie off her feet and carried her to the dining table. I carefully pushed the paper to the floor and laid her across the table. I stood between her legs and massaged her torso. I'd drawn an imaginary line from her navel to her womanhood with my fingertips. I removed her panties and pressed my thumb gently against her center, applying just the right amount of pressure. Her clit protested against my fingers. The heat rose yet again. Lexie's back arched to my touch. With my tongue, I retraced the line from her breasts to her womanhood, planting soft, moist kisses along the way. A groan rumbled from her core and escaped through her lips. I left Lexie on the table for a brief moment in search of ice. I invited maple syrup to the party. I placed one of the ice cubes in my mouth and began nibbling on her nipples. Lexie arched her back again and released a sweet gurgle. My intention was to lead her to the brink of desire. I paid special attention to spots that triggered the most pleasing response. I circled her breasts again with the ice in my hand, kissing her sporadically. I made my way down to her love canal, massaging her breasts, sides and bottom. Her sweet essence filled my nostrils. I pulled her closer to the edge of the table by her waist. Taking her legs into my hands, I circled my tongue around her sweetness and slowly penetrated her womanhood with my tongue, lapping at her steady flow of juices. She was delectable. I slipped into a rhythm. Lexie released melodic cries of ecstasy. She moved her pelvis in sync with my tongue. We moved together until rapture rocked her body. I poured on the maple syrup, licking, sucking and tasting until the sweetness dissipated and her juices flowed more feverishly. She arched higher, trembled and cried out, releasing everything. I played in her juices with my tongue until she could no longer stand it and collapsed flat back against the table. She reached for me and pulled me in close and held on for dear life.

"Oh Brian," she whispered repeatedly.

Lexie turned the tables on me. I was now her prey. Lexie led me to the chair and removed my clothing with slow persistence.

Once naked she sat me on the couch and examined me as if to figure out where she should start. On her knees, her lustful smile amplified my passion. Lexie touched me everywhere, acquainting herself with my body. She ran her fingers over my head and held me by the nape of my neck, bestowing a gentle erotic massage. She straddled me. I could feel her wetness. She kissed me slowly, grinding backwards and forwards. She then made her way down my torso to my beseeching manhood. Lexie meticulously poured syrup around my penis and placed an ice chip in her mouth. Playfully she planted soft wet kisses along the crease of my pelvis. Her movements sparked a pleasing sensation throughout my body.

Lexie's hands cupped my backside as she pulled me to her, teasing the tip and walls of my penis with her icy tongue. With the tightened tip of her tongue she grazed the underside of my penis, evoking violent waves of pleasure. I was close to climaxing without so much as oral penetration. With an incredible suctioning motion, she surrounded my penis with the warm moist walls of her mouth, exercising an urgent rhythm. My eyes rolled up into my head. She gently jerked me as she performed this spectacular act. Lexie proceeded to drive me to the ends of the earth with a milking sensation. I wanted to yell for her to stop but I couldn't speak. My back involuntarily arched and my eyes grew wild. My toes curled from the immense pleasure. I lifted her head and kissed her with such intensity, releasing pleasure-filled moans into her mouth. I stood lifting her with me and laid her face up on the couch.

On my knees in front of the couch, I placed her legs over my shoulders and entered her. She moaned in delight. I began with deep, controlled strokes. The walls of her vagina closed in on me, pulling me in for more. I held a steady rhythm and gradually

71

increased the pace and intensity. With a firm hold on her bountiful breasts, I stroked meaningfully, squeezing tighter as the heat rose within me. Lexie grabbed the sides of my thighs and pulled me in deeper. We rode in unison until our juices overflowed. Our bodies tightened and released together. We shuddered simultaneously collapsing into one another. We came down together. Lexie massaged the nape of my neck. We remained silent for what seemed like eternity. It was just like I imagined it would be.

"Brian," Lexie said softly.

"Oh, now you want to talk to me? I suppose you want to cuddle too?"

We burst out laughing. It felt good. I could have never joked like that with crazy Shelly.

"You know, you need to take your show on the road," Lexie joked. "Really," she continued, "seriously."

"Okay, Lexie, what's up?"

"I don't..." she paused. "I don't want to seem like the silly overzealous girl that assumes everything is supposed to change because of a little sex."

"Talk to me," I said as I sat up to face her and offer comfort in knowing that it was not just about sex to me either.

"Well partner, I want to know where your head is at with this. Just promise me that whatever happens, we go with the flow. No forced-feeding."

"No forced-feeding."

I held up my right hand like a boy scout.

"Good, I won't pressure you," Lexie said and sighed.

This felt right. A few minutes passed and I figured that this was as good a time as any to let her know about my trip. I looked down at Lexie still lying on her back and decided to tell her right then. When I found the words, she was sound asleep. I carried her to her bedroom, covered her naked body, and kissed her on the forehead.

"Good night partner," I whispered and left.

Lexie   CHAPTER 11

The night with Brian was incredible. I knew it would happen one
day, but didn't know when. I wanted to make sure that David was
completely out of my system. When I thought about the time Brian
and I shared, my legs would tremble and the hairs on my arms
would stand on end. Brian was incredible in bed. I was determined
to take things slowly with him.

Brian called me at work and asked that we meet after work for
drinks because he needed to talk. I hoped it wasn't anything about
Shelly. As far as I was concerned, she was out of her mind. I must
admit, now that I've experienced Brian in bed, I know why she
acted so crazy. All of a sudden, I pitied the girl. Unfortunately, I was
not about to let him get away, especially after the masterful way in
which he strummed my chords.

I was so tired I could hardly keep my eyes open, especially
after such a sleepless night. If the boss called one more meeting, I
swear I was going home sick. It was close to the end of the day and
I needed to get myself together before meeting with Brian. My
phone rang and startled me.

"Alexia Mitchell."

"What's up, partner?"

Brian had one hell of a deep, smooth voice. You could bathe

in its depth.

"Hey partner, where are we going for drinks?"

My body shuddered at the memory of the great sex we shared. Goose bumps blanketed my arms. Luckily no one passed my office. My body shook like I climaxed all over again. I grunted. Damn!

"What was that?" Brian asked.

"Nothing," I chuckled. I couldn't believe I grunted so loudly.

"Let's meet at Houlihan's on Forty-Second Street," he suggested

"Sounds great! I'll see you in about an hour, partner."

Houlihan's was extremely crowded. I sat close to the door so that Brian would see me as soon as he walked in. I ordered myself an apple martini to get started. It tasted great. A little of the cocktail made its way down my chin. I tried to be discreet in a very ladylike manner and wipe it off before anyone saw anything. I turned to get a napkin. By the time my eyes made it back to the door to see if Brian had arrived, I was clutching my mouth to avoid spitting my drink out and spraying innocent bystanders. I held my throat and forced myself to swallow the remaining contents. I coughed to keep from choking when I saw that David was standing right next to me. He reached over, handed me another napkin and patted my back.

"Are you okay?"

"Fine," I gasped.

"What's up, you surprised to see me?"

Please don't think I am falling all over the place because of you, asshole. "A little of my drink went down the wrong pipe. That's all." I rolled my eyes.

David didn't look that great for some reason. He was always together, but this time he wasn't quite himself.

"Well, how have you been?" he asked leaning his elbows on

75

the high table.

"Fine. And you?"

Before he could answer, I interrupted, "You know, I am waiting for a friend who should be here any minute now. I don't want him to get the wrong impression."

"What, I can't talk to you in public anymore?"

David looked at me like he wanted to slap me.

"David, I didn't say that to upset you." *Yes I did.* "It's just that I'm waiting on someone."

"Well, when you are done with your friend, I would like to talk to you." He glared at me.

"Maybe we can meet up and talk some other time."

I tried to keep from getting upset myself. The nerve of this bastard! He acted as if I owed his ass something. He was the one that dogged me out.

I spotted Brian looking around trying to find me.

"Please excuse me," I said to David as calmly as I could then pushed past him to get to Brian.

I felt like I was losing my breath. I wanted to grab Brian and tongue him down right there at the door in front of David. I decided at the very last minute to act like a lady just say 'hello.' Then I took notice of Brian. He looked as smooth as I have ever remembered seeing him. A wicked little smile spread across my face. I took hold of Brian's arm to lead him away. When I looked back at David he was arguing with the same woman I caught him screwing in his apartment a few months back. I hadn't noticed her before but assumed she wasn't happy about seeing David and me talking.

Finally we were seated and suddenly I was starving. That apple martini and David had gotten to my head and I needed to eat something fast. I ordered food and a glass of Chardonnay with my meal. We engaged only in small talk once the food arrived.

"What's on your mind?" Brian asked me.

"Why?"

"Because, you seem distracted."

"Oh, I'm sorry, I had a long day at work," I lied.

"Good," Brian said with a look of relief.

"Why, good?" I was confused.

"I thought you were uneasy about what happened last night."

Was he crazy?

"To tell you the truth, I really enjoyed last night. I thought a lot about it today. Now I know why Shelly acts so crazy!" I burst out laughing.

Apparently Brian didn't think it was as funny as I did. He didn't laugh at all. I stopped and apologized for laughing and tried to change the subject.

"You're looking pretty sharp today. What's up with that?" I asked.

"Oh, I finished with my consulting assignment today. I always dress like this for work. Brian paused and started again, "Listen I need to tell you something."

His uneasiness made me nervous, and I downed a huge gulp of my wine a little too quickly. I nearly choked again, and again there was wine dripping along my chin. Damn!"

"Is everything all right?" I asked. I felt the urge to leave right then and there.

"No everything is cool," he said and paused. "It's been a long time since I had to say something to a woman and was at a loss for words."

Butterflies took flight in my abdomen.

"It's me, Brian—just let it out," I said as calmly as I could.

I really didn't know what to expect. As we ate, Brian talked about how he felt for me but wanted to keep his feelings at bay because of the situation with David. When he said David's name I swallowed hard, hoping it went unnoticed. I was over David. Yet for some reason his presence in the same restaurant made me uncomfortable. The last thing I wanted was a scene. Then Brian dropped the bomb. He explained that last night he actually came over to have this conversation with me and proceeded to tell me how I had three months to get ready for him. The following Monday, he would be leaving to embark on a three month excursion.

"Something, something, blah, blah, blah," was all I heard after the three-month trip. I was stuck on stupid. I didn't hear anything else. Just when things began to turn around, this curve ball was thrown my way. I couldn't believe this. I ordered another drink. Something stronger than chardonnay but I can't recall what it was.

"Brian, why haven't you told me about your trip before?"

Brian was leaving in less than two weeks. How was I supposed to handle this? As I had done so many times before, I asked myself, "Why me?" As soon as I get a grip on something good in life, it gets snatched away from me.

"Lexie, I don't know. I wanted to talk about it, but I didn't know how to bring it up."

"How long have you been planning this trip?"

"I have been saving up for years. I just needed the time. I started planning a few weeks ago, since I realized my consulting assignment would end earlier than I expected. Now I have the money and the time."

"Wow Brian, I don't know what to say."

I shook my head to absorb the reality.

"Listen, I'm not finished," Brian looked up at the ceiling. After a pause that seemed to last forever he spoke again. "I want you, Lexie. I don't want to play any games with you. But I didn't think I could ask you to wait for me. This is something I wanted to do all my life and now I have the chance. So I had to come to terms with meeting the woman that I knew I could make mine for good, at a time when I would have to walk away from her before we ever got a chance to really get started."

Oh, Lord! I couldn't believe my ears. I was stunned. Everything I ever felt for Brian came rushing to the surface. I closed my eyes and pictured myself walking down the street with him in Paris.

"Maybe you think I was wrong, but I didn't know a better way. This is my conclusion, the game plan. You have three months to get ready for me. Sow your little oats and get all the guys out of your system, because when I get back it's all about you and me. I can't account for what happens when I'm gone, but I want you to consider us a done deal when I return. Just you and me, partner! I need to know if that's what you want too."

Utter shock and sheer happiness was what I felt. I didn't have a response. I just sat dumbfounded. I wanted this too and missed him already. I grabbed our passing waiter and asked for the check.

Brian   CHAPTER 12

Lexie and I had spent almost every waking moment together since I told her about my trip. First she didn't know how to act. Then she started asking me a thousand questions about where I would stay. What I would do and if I would get lonely? What would I do when I started feeling horny? We even discussed Lexie coming to visit if she could get the time.

I had been planning this trip forever. I told Lexie not to worry and that I would be okay. I had learned as much French, Spanish and Italian as I would need to get by. I was renting a small studio apartment in London that would serve as home base while I was there. I got that hook-up from an ex-coworker who had family there. I planned to spend at least one week in London, getting familiar with the place and then taking a few days here and there, visiting as many European countries as I possibly could. It worked to be much cheaper to get a place in London and arrange my trips from there as opposed to trying to set everything up from here. Over the next couple of weeks I would spend time hopping from country to country, stopping back at home base periodically.

Before returning home I would have experienced life in France, Italy, Greece, Spain, Morocco and wherever else I could visit. I planned to spend anywhere from a few days to about a week in each place. I had not planned on staying at any five-star hotels or ritzy resorts. My excursion would only include the likes of places comparable to the Days Inn and Howard Johnson. This would be a trip that I would remember for the rest of my life. My mom told me to make sure I sent her a postcard from each place I went. She had never even been on an airplane before and though she was thrilled about my plans, she still couldn't believe I was finally going through with it. Mom promised to take care of my place while I was away.

It was time to go. I called Mom to say goodbye. She made me stay on the line for a quick prayer before saying farewell and bidding me a safe trip. I was good and tired. I had been running all day taking care of last minute things. Lexie even left work early to help out. It was now after six p.m. and my flight was scheduled to leave at nine. I would arrive at the London, Heathrow airport at nine the next morning. I looked around the apartment one last time to see if I had everything.

The only thing I regret leaving behind is Lexie. She had that look in her eyes. I dropped my bags, grabbed her by the hand and led her to the couch. I was already starting to sweat and had only begun to touch her. Lexie held me tight while we kissed, long and hard. When we finished the kiss, we were both out of breath. Lexie stared me right in my eyes as she slid down in front of me and unbuckled my jeans. By the time she got through the belt and zipper my man was as hard as a role of quarters. Lexie pulled him out and kissed him.

"I'm gonna miss you man," she said to my penis.

Lexie   CHAPTER 13

I missed Brian and I was also mad at him. A week had past since he left and I hadn't heard from him yet. So much for, "when I get back it's all about you and me." No call, no postcard, no e-mail, nothing. Since this was my time to "sow my oats" I figured I may as well get to "sowing." Dante had called twice and Brooke wanted to hang out too. It was time to get out and have some fun. I was going to have good time as if my life depended on it. Forget about Brian. Who was I fooling? I was hurt. Empty promises, I had fallen for them again.

I'll party when the weekend gets here but for now I need long, hot, soothing bath. Today was a long day at work. The bosses love me and my team is performing well. I've done nothing but exceed all of my goals and objectives since getting my promotion. I made my bosses shine. As far as work is concerned, life is good.

Just as I placed my big toe in the hot, bubbly, sweet-smelling water my damn doorbell rang. I developed an instant attitude. Then I thought about it. Brooke was supposed to come by and pick up a book that we had to read for our next book club meeting. It had to be her. I threw on my silk robe without even tying it and ran to the door.

"Goodness, girl, I'm coming!" I yelled.

Brooke and David always rang the bell too many times.

Neither of them had much patience. It was Brooke all right, ringing and knocking at the same time. I flung the door open and headed back for the bathroom.

"It's right on the kitchen table. I was just getting in the tub." I shouted.

"Lexie."

When I heard David's voice I halted, took a deep breath, pulled my robe together, and turned around very slowly. David stepped in and closed the door. I was at a loss for words. What did he want?

"Hello David. What brings you here?"

"Well…"

"RINGING MY DAMN BELL LIKE A MADMAN!" I shouted, interrupting him.

"Whoa, Lexie. Chill a moment," David said with his hands in the air in mock surrender.

I wanted to walk away but I was in my own house. What the hell did he want anyway? This is just want I needed, like a whole in my damn head.

"Please make it snappy, Dave. I was just about to take a much needed and well deserved bath," I snapped.

"I won't keep you too long. Can I at least have a seat?" he asked.

"Sure, Dave. Sit!" It sounded like I was talking to a dog. Then it dawned on me, I was. The thought made me giggle. I remained in the same spot with my arms folded. I wasn't really mad at Dave anymore. I just didn't feel like being nice to him.

"Aren't you going to sit?" he asked.

"I wasn't planning on it. I was about to take a bath, remember?" I rolled my eyes for effect and then snickered to myself.

"Just be civilized for a moment and let's talk like adults,

please," Dave pleaded.

"Fine."

I spun around to head over to the couch, not realizing that the strap to my robe had fallen. When I spun around, the strap under my foot caused me to slip and fall flat back on my behind with my legs ajar. All of my business was out in the open as I sat stark naked, on top of my half open robe. Dave's eyes and mouth were wide open. I couldn't believe that I had fallen right there in front of him. Then he quickly covered his mouth with his hand and looked away. I felt embarrassed, which quickly dissipated. Here I was trying to be sassy and show attitude, and now I lay on my butt with all of my goods on display.

Dave tried his best not to laugh. I just sat there and closed my robe.

"Well what did you want to talk about?" I asked, still lying on the floor.

Dave looked at me, startled. "Aren't you going to get up"

After that he couldn't hold it in anymore. Dave burst out laughing and so did I. Then Dave helped me up. I told him to go ahead and have a seat while I go to the bathroom to get my cup of tea. I decided to put on a tank and some sweats. I didn't want Dave getting any ideas. He had already seen enough. When I came back into the room, Dave was looking at the pictures that I had set out. There were pictures of Brooke, my family, Brian, and me. Dave looked at the pictures of Brian really hard. He must have remembered him from Houlihan's that night. I started to offer him something to drink but decided against it.

"Well dearest Dave, what brings you here tonight?" I said with all the sarcasm I could muster.

"I screwed up," he came right out with it.

"Oh you did, did you?" I mocked. "Really David, you don't have to explain, especially after all this time," I said and took a seat on my sofa.

"Yes I do. Lexie, I haven't been happy since you left. I know I was wrong but I miss you. Look at what we had—you mean to tell me that all of that accounted for nothing? I wanted to marry you."

I pretended to gag. David sighed.

"David, please. Stop it while you're ahead."

"I realize that I still care for you," he said, looking pitiful.

"So what is that supposed to mean now, Dave? As a matter of fact, aren't you still with the same girl that you were screwing when this all began?"

"I was but it's not the same Lexie—she's not you."

"She sure as hell isn't! But she made a fine substitute that day you had her ass hiked up on your desk. Why is it that she isn't good enough now, David?"

"Lexie, you don't understand...I,"

"What is there to understand David? Understand what? That you were being doggish? That you wanted to have your cake and eat it too but got caught? My plane hadn't prepared for take-off and you were on to the next woman. The best part of it was that you weren't even man enough to face me after the bullshit that you pulled and you shipped my belongings to me as if I was in another state. How about you understand this, Dave? I am past all of that. I have moved on. I am so sick of you thirsty-ass men realizing what you've lost long after the well has run dry. Here is some advice for the future—realize what you've got before it's gone. As far as you and I are concerned, we are done. Get over it!"

Dave dropped his head.

"I miss our friendship. I still want to be friends. Is that too much to ask?" he asked.

I walked to the door and opened it. "Goodnight Dave."

David got up very slowly and walked to the door.

"You'll break, I'll get you back," he said.

I chuckled sarcastically as he passed though the door then I slammed it as hard as I possibly could.

Suddenly I was mad at Brian all over again.

The doorbell rang again. I swung it open, screaming like a mad woman.

"I don't believe you," I screamed and looked up into Brooke's face.

"Damn, girl! What got your panties in bunch? I guess I know since I just saw David leave. What on earth did he want?" Brooke asked, walking into the apartment. I closed the door behind her.

"Girl you won't believe what I have been through in the past couple of days." I said and told Brooke to have a seat while I checked my bath water. I retrieved the book she came for and poured two glasses of wine. I had every intention of getting my bath. I just had to take some time to share the happenings with my girl. I told Brooke all about the Brian and David ordeals. Before I knew it, Brooke had me in stitches with her own accounts and personal take on my situation. I also shared with the Brooke the story about Ronald 'Stinky-Man' Covington. Brooke was in awe, covering her mouth with her hand as I revealed the details of that eventful evening.

"Girl I can't believe that man brought you back to his place with his stinking ass trying to get some. Now you know he was"—

together we chimed—"Dead WRONG." Our bodies shook from our gut-wrenching laughter.

"Now Lexie, how am I supposed to face this man when I get back to work tomorrow, knowing his ass smells and he has skid marks in his boxers?" We continued to crack up. "I am going to have to try my damnedest to keep from saying, 'What's up, Stinky?' Maybe I should buy some underwear and put them in his office before he gets to work in the morning," she joked.

I had tears streaming down my cheeks.

"Brooke, you're a mess. Now cut it out because I know you and your silly ass would do just that. Just leave that stinking-assed man alone. He doesn't even know the real reason why I ran out like that. He still thinks I had stomach problems."

Brooke thought back and said, "No wonder that fool asked if you were feeling better when I saw him at work the next week. I should just tell him you developed a bad case of 'smell-a-stink-ass-itis.'" Brooke roared.

Still laughing I told Brooke she had to go. She was making my stomach hurt and it was time for my bath. Brooke prepared to leave and left me her final thought about my life.

"I know Brian seems like a good catch, but don't get all caught up in the prospect when that fool may never make it back to the states. Live your life and whatever will be, will be. You know you don't need to add undue stress to your life, banking on possibilities. And that's the truth, because you know I never lie!"

I assured Brooke I had everything under control, told her I loved her and kicked her out so that I could get into my highly antic-ipated bath.

Brian　　　　　　　　CHAPTER I4

London is amazing. The neighborhood where I rented my studio reminds me a little of downtown Brooklyn. There are a lot of black people in the area—most of them from the islands. I must admit that it did serve as some sort of comfort. I don't feel like I'm far from home. My studio is small but nice and very cozy. It came furnished with a view. I paid my rent for the three months upon my arrival.

During the first week I mapped out my game plan for my travels. I met a girl, Heather, who promised to show me the town. Heather introduced me to two of her friends, Lyn, short for Marilyn, and Zette, short for Lizette, who were also willing to help me feel at home. They took me out on the town. We went to a nice West Indian restaurant downtown that played live reggae music. The atmosphere was toxic. The three of them drank so much I felt like the girl in the group. Remembering that I was the one from out of town, I didn't want to get too intoxicated or put too much trust into anyone yet. The girls showed me a great time.

The first two weeks they took great care of me. They showed me how to get around. We went clubbing, checked out local restaurants and bars, and went sight seeing. I hit every famous tourist area imaginable, from castles and palaces to the jazz and blues clubs in their neighborhood called Soho. They also made dinner for me several times. Heather let me call my mother from her house because my cell phone would not work. I wanted to call Lexie, but not from her house. Heather was a little nosy and hung on to every word I said. I called to get my own phone put in but had to wait well over a week to get it connected. I decided not to leave London until I was all set up with my own telephone line and all.

When my phone was finally connected, I called Lexie to let her know how things were going. At first it sounded like she was trying to give me attitude. Sensing this, I explained what I had to go through to get a phone and told her about my cell phone not working. After that, she appeared to be happy to hear from me. She told me about David coming over with some bullshit. I didn't pay much attention to that because I just didn't want to hear about him. I explained to her that I would be leaving in a few days to head over to France, my second stop on this excursion. I told her that I would give her a call whenever I got back to London, although I wouldn't be spending much more time there. She sounded sad. I was happy because I knew that meant she missed me. I closed the call by telling her to "keep it tight" and she asked me if I got horny yet. I told her to just concentrate on having her fun now because when I got back it would all be over. I felt her smile. For a minute I wished I were home.

That weekend, before heading to France, Heather, Lyn, and Zette took me out to a restaurant called Kensington Place. The food was excellent and the atmosphere was great. Although I didn't see anyone that night, Kensington Place was supposedly known to be a celebrity hot spot. After we left the restaurant we went to a nice club called the Blue Note. We were actually going to another spot but changed our minds when we saw a bunch of young kids hang-ing out front waiting to get in. It was one of the few places where you could hear hip-hop, but you also had to face the crowd and none of us were in the mood. It had three levels that played differ-ent music so you could vibe to whatever you were feeling at the moment. The girls drank like fish and got plastered. Heather was the designated driver, so she kept her intake to a minimum.

We left the Blue Note earlier than I expected. Heather insist-ed that we go to her place for a few more drinks instead of going straight home. She was slightly tipsy yet able to maintain her stature. I wasn't feeling too badly myself. I was at a point where I trusted the girls a little more. Once we arrived at Heather's she pulled out some kind of Russian Vodka and put on some R&B. We were chilling when Zette, who was wasted by now, decided it was too hot in the apartment and started stripping. I just sat there and watched until she was down to her bra, panties and a soft pink camisole. She had a fat ass. Her face was okay, but that ass was her most abundant asset. At first Heather looked a little embarrassed, but Zette didn't care. She kept dancing and grooving to the music with her drink in her hand. She didn't miss a beat. Heather relaxed a little. Lyn couldn't stop giggling.

"Zette, girl, how are you just going to sit here and take off your bloody clothes like that?" Lyn asked.

"It's hot in here. You know you want to take your clothes off too."

"I can't believe you women," Heather said and shook her head, laughing as well.

Actually, I was feeling good and wouldn't have minded if the rest of them took off their clothes. As far as I was concerned, we could have an orgy up in here. I got up and started dancing with Zette. Still holding her drink she put her other hand up on my shoulder and started a winding dance moving up and down.

"Yeah!" I shouted and started laughing.

"Wait right there." Zette said. She went over to the radio, turned it up, started dancing back towards my direction and began removing her remaining garments. This time my manhood said, "yeah," standing at complete attention. It didn't take much with the amount of liquor we all managed to consume. Zette was in front of me, naked, dancing like she was fully clothed, back at the Blue Note. She turned her back to me. I grabbed her tits from behind and began a slowly grinding her on her backside. Heather's eyes almost popped out of her face, and Lyn was now laughing hysterically. I thought she was about to hyperventilate.

Zette and I continued dancing and feeling on each other as if we were alone. Zette closed her eyes and kept grooving. Then she turned to me without skipping a beat, and with the same rhythm, unbuttoned my shirt, then my pants. We were dancing face to face. Zette's hand made its way up and down my chest and around to my ass as she pulled me closer to her with every beat. There we were still dancing, touching one another everywhere we could reach. My shirt was hanging off my shoulders and my pants and boxers were at my ankles. Zette danced completely naked, her underwear thrown around the area. We were having a ball. She danced with my manhood to the rhythm of the music. I touched and teased her from head to toe.

Lyn looked like she wanted to join us but couldn't stop giggling. Finally her lust got the better of her, and she began fondling herself. She moved to the music. Heather didn't know what to do

91

with herself besides stare back and forth from Zette and me to Lyn in the chair feeling herself. I invited Heather to join the party.

"You guys have your fun. I'm having enough fun watching."

Heather sat back and enjoyed the show. The more she drank, the more relaxed she became. But she still refused to join us. Eventually she went in to her room to retrieve a couple of condoms, anticipating that the real party was about to get started.

Lyn joined us on the dance floor. I helped her remove her clothes until she was completely naked. One in the front and one in the back, we danced for the longest time. Eventually we had to move on the next possible step. Heather threw the condoms from across the room. I strummed Lyn's vaginal cords as we swayed to the music. Without missing a beat, Zette secured my manhood with a condom and gently played along the tip. She took him into her mouth as far as he could go. It felt sensual even through rubber. While Zette sucked, I kissed Lyn's breast and rolled her clit between my fingers. She was dripping wet, still giggling. Zette bent over reached through her legs and guided my penis into her. Lyn looked lost for a minute because there was not much for her to do, so she started kissing Zette. Zette turned Lyn over and took her clit into her mouth, while I continued to grind deeper into her from behind.

Heather simply observed the show while sipping her vodka. She occasionally offered a sly smile. Zette came hard, racking her body with ripples of pleasure and then she changed places with Lyn. I put on a new condom and entered Lyn. Lyn was a little tighter and I knew I wouldn't last too long. Lyn moved well and together we establish an erotic, rhythmic blend. We rode the wave until we climaxed in unison. The three of us lay on the floor attempting to slow our breathing, still laughing.

"Damn, Heather. What kind of heat do you use in this place? I need another drink," Zette said and walked over to the table. She drank straight from the bottle.

I told the ladies goodnight and thanked them for such an interesting evening.

"Hit and run, do you?" Zette teased. We all shared a good laugh.

Heather offered to drive me home. I politely declined and told her I could use the walk. Besides, my studio was only a few short blocks away. I kissed Heather on her forehead and told her I would see her before I left.

"Get some sleep, I'll bring you breakfast," she said, then smiled and shook her head.

Lexie   CHAPTER 15

Dante called me again and asked to go out for dinner. After avoiding him I finally accepted. This time we went to Jimmy's Downtown, which is actually in midtown. We had a good time but Dante was completely full of himself and it was getting on my nerves. It seemed like he was checking out every woman to see if she was looking at him. He did look good, but he was much too preoccupied with himself. Although dinner was nice, I made a mental note not to go out with him again.

Part of my reason for not fully enjoying the evening was because of Brian. I found myself constantly thinking about him. I really admired the idea of his trip and thought it took a lot of courage. But our conversation that night at Houlihan's kept replaying itself in my head. I still couldn't get past the point where he actually made a claim for me and left me hanging. I know I care for him, but I am not convinced that he's going to come back and sweep me off of my feet like a knight in shining armor destined to live happily ever after with me.

I can't help thinking "out of sight, out of mind." I could just see Brian coming back and acting like I dreamed this whole idea up on my own. A part of me really wanted it to come true and another part of me was convinced that it wasn't going to happen. The truth is I really wanted to settle down. I was getting too old for the single's scene. I thought David would be the one that I would marry until I caught him screwing the other woman. Now after all is said and done, I am kind of glad that whole thing happened. If not, I would have never met Brian, and I believe Brian is really the one.

I tried my best to enjoy the rest of the evening and even let Dante' kiss me when he dropped me home. I called Brooke. You can always count on Brooke to tell it like it is. Basically she said for me to stop tripping and live my life, enjoy myself and have fun regardless of what tomorrow might bring. She said that Brian was probably over there getting all the European women he could handle, while I was here sitting around thinking about him.

"Didn't he tell you to sow your oats? If he comes back for you like a knight in shinning armor, then hell, go with the flow, Cinderella," Brooke advised.

Brooke was right. I was tripping. I agreed to hang out with Dante again and take time to work things out.

During the next week, I came home to a package from Brian, addressed from a gallery in France. I couldn't wait to get it open. He sent a note with it.

Lexie,

What's up, partner? Are you keeping it tight for me? (Smile) While in France I ran across a small gallery event and saw this painting. It reminded me of you, and I remembered that you love abstract art, so I bought it for you. I hope you like it. It's an original. I will be head-ing to Italy for a week before heading back to London. I will call you when I get back home. We really need to talk about out visiting me at some point. That would be nice. I hope you like the painting. Take

care and remember, when I get back it's on! Ha!
    Peace partner,
    B.

The painting was absolutely gorgeous. Damn, Brian really knows my taste. I had to find somewhere to put it. It definitely had to go in the living room. I would love to visit Brian, but I just can't get the time right now. Things are getting critical at work. They need me there. Besides, Brian will be home in a couple of weeks. Or maybe I could get to him over a weekend when he gets back to London. Now that sounds like a possibility.

I felt better and decided to call Dante and see what he was up to. I obviously called him at a bad time because a woman picked up the phone with an attitude from hell.

"HELLO?"

I was about to hang up but decided against it.

"Hello, may I speak to Dante?"

"Who the fuck is this?" The girl asked. "What's up with the bitches calling, Dante?"

I listened to them fight for while. I was getting a kick out of it.

"Don't answer my phone like that. Do I do that shit to you?" Dante scolded.

"I don't have other guys calling my house!"

"That's your choice. Now give me my damn phone. You had no business answering it. Did I ask you to answer my phone? Huh?"

"You make me sick," was apparently the only thing she could come up with.

"Hello," Dante finally said to me.

"Hi Dante, I obviously called at a bad time. How about you

call me back later?"

"What's up Lexie? You don't have to call back—she was just leaving."

I could hear her in the background, "Oh I was just leaving, was I? You know what I am out of here. I don't have the patience for you and your games anymore. You're a cheap ass anyway."

The door slammed so hard I jumped on my end of the phone.

"Wow!," was all I could say.

"Don't pay that any mind. She's crazy. I wanna know what's going on with you," Dante said.

I couldn't do anything but laugh. Dante and I talked for a while and he offered to take me out again. I gave him an excuse about work dominating my schedule and told him I would get back to him sometime soon. I would hate to run into that woman he was arguing with.

Over the next few weeks I continued to get gifts from places throughout Europe: perfume from France, a designer bag from Italy and chocolates from Belgium and Germany. Brian and I spoke briefly whenever he stopped back in London. I enjoyed the gifts and notes he sent. Labor Day had just passed which meant Brian would be home in less than three weeks.

Just before lunch, the bosses called an emergency meeting. I assumed there was something going on with the competition. Whenever our competitors launch a new product or program, we get together in an emergency meeting which was more like a strategy session to determine how we would respond in the market. The senior vice president wanted to see the entire department—all of marketing. However this wasn't a strategy session: we were all being let go. My boss, our staff and half the sales force and administrative assistants. Even Shari lost her job. She cried, and I felt horrible for her. Although she didn't make much, she was a dedicated employee. She was also a single mom with beer money and champagne taste.

What would the executives do without their assistants? I could not believe what I was hearing. Everything after "I'm sorry" was a blur. Layoff! The first thing I thought of was what I would do when I woke up in the morning and had no place to go. I felt like I had lost control and was sinking in quicksand. We were all asked to clear out our desks, files and computers. I absently went through the motions. The office was in total chaos. People were crying all over the place saying their good byes. I didn't take it personally.

My boss, Mary Ann, came into my office to see how I was doing. I could tell she had been crying. Mary Ann had been with the company since she graduated from college. Comtel was all she had ever known. Mary Ann wasn't crying about the money, she had plenty of that. She was upset because her life was being altered without her input. She told me if there was anything at all that she could do for me that I was to let her know right away. She said she enjoyed working with me and she reassured me that I would survive with or without Comtel because I knew how to adapt. Mary Ann hugged me and said a sobbing goodbye.

I had no idea where to go. I thought I should go home first and get my head together. I arranged to have my personal belongings shipped to my house and went out to lunch with Shari. When I went home that night I rearranged my living room. I wasn't worried about money because I had built up a considerable rainy-day reserve. That's one thing that my mom preached. My savings was enough to keep me afloat for a few months, so I decided to take some time to myself before starting to look for another job. It felt so odd to be unemployed. I wasn't angry or depressed, just numb.

I called my sisters, Brooke, some other associates and prior co-workers to let them know my new job status in case they came across anything. I wanted to get away but had no place to go. I longed for a note, gift or some token from Brian.

Brian called me. He was back in London for the next few days. I told him about the layoff.

"Good you were due for a vacation. Now you can come and visit me for a week," he said.

He was absolutely right. I decided right then and there that I would go. We spoke about meeting in London and he would take me with him on his next journey. The only drawback was that I had to be in London within the next two days. Brian wouldn't tell me where we would go from there. He only said to get a round trip between London and New York and whatever happened from there would be his surprise. This was just what I needed. I was ready to go.

I felt a little bit of relief. I truly needed to get away. Ever since I received my promotion I worked extra hard for that company every day, no days off, no vacation, nothing! It was my time. I would make the best use of it. Maybe consult and work my own hours, but this was not the time to think about that. I needed to focus on what I was going to wear in Europe. I had to go shopping. Besides, in addition to my savings, I had a nice bit of change coming to me as part of my severance package. A little shopping trip to ease the pain wouldn't hurt. I promised myself that I wouldn't do any major damage.

I thought about my life over the past year and it reminded me about my mother's saying about the two shades of blue. The first shade was the promising blue of a clear sky on a beautiful sunny day. The shade that makes you feel good inside, the shade you feel when your life is going well. Then there is the flip side, the dark, murky blue that you feel when life decides to remind you that everything can't always be rosy. This past year has just been one big roller coaster ride, filled with mountain highs and valley lows. Just when everything is going great, my clear blue skies turn dark and murky. I felt it deep down inside, the blues. David, my job, what next? Brian? Sometimes I couldn't see the joy in things because I know the blues will not be far behind.

Brian   CHAPTER 16

I'm looking forward to seeing Lexie. It's been a long time since I've seen her smile. Not to mention, even though I'm having the experience of a lifetime, I am getting a little homesick. I want some of my mother's macaroni and cheese with some fried chicken so badly, I can taste it. A part of me can't wait to get home. Maybe when Lexie gets here I will ask her to make some soul food for me before we head off on our little expedition.

101

I had already started to plan the agenda for Lexie's visit. We would spend a few days in Paris and take a tour of Italy. By then it would be time for her to return to New York. I wanted to show her a good time and make her forget about her job situation. Even though she acts like it doesn't bother her, I know she has to be more affected by this layoff than what she lets on. Lexie put a lot of time and energy into that job and was very proud of it.

I wondered if I should introduce her to the girls. Actually I don't think that would be a good idea. I don't need the drama, and women are capable of anything. We won't be here long enough anyway, so it doesn't make a difference. Besides, I don't need any interruptions when Lexie gets here. We need to make up for lost time. I wanted to get Lexie a little gift or something for when she arrives. I thought about checking out this little lingerie shop, until I remembered I really didn't care for that stuff anyway. I thought it got in the way. I'd rather see Lexie butt-ass naked. Plus I'm sure she will bring plenty of stock on her own. I settled on a bottle of wine and made reservations for a nice restaurant. I guess if I am going to ask her to cook for me, the least I could do is show her a nice time when she first gets here.

Speaking of Ma's home cooking it was time to give her a call. I keep in touch with her mostly when I am here in London.

"What's up, Ma? How's my main lady doing?"

"I am just fine. How's my baby doing out there in those funny talking' places?"

"Pretty good, Ma. What's new with you?"

"Not much 'cept that damn sister of mine getting on my nerves"

"What's Aunt Liz up to now?"

"Just being a pain in the butt. She complains 'bout my cooking, saying everything I cook is fattening. I told her ass, don't eat nothin' I cook. I betcha every time she walk in my house she take her narrow ass straight to the fridge. You know she can't cook."

I laughed because I could see the two of them. Ma was a down-home cook and Aunt Liz was one of those women stuck on a health kick. She ate no red meat and everything she cooked was bland. Even though she gets on my mother nerves, she loves her cooking.

"Well Ma, you know Aunt Liz."

"You're right, that's my sister. Now you get off this phone. I know this call is gonna cost you. You take care of yourself out there and give me a call again soon."

"Okay. Oh, Lexie is coming to visit me for a few days."

"Oh really, well that's nice. I like that girl. Speaking of which, why you don't…"

"Ma!"

"Okay, I'll leave it alone. I just want you to be happy and get a girl you can settle down with and she seems nice."

"I love you Ma. Take care of yourself. I will be home sooner than you think."

"All right baby. Do something with yourself while you're out there with that girl like get married and make some babies or something," she howled after that last comment. I couldn't help but laugh at how she tried to slip that in.

"Later lady, I love you. And remember if you need me just call me collect."

"Bye, baby."

I love that woman. She had spunk, was down to earth and funny, and no one I knew could match her skills in the kitchen. I felt like a child anticipating Christmas. I was really looking forward to seeing Lexie and couldn't get past my excitement. She took a night flight and would be in at nine o'clock tomorrow morning. I had to do something with myself but couldn't think of anything.

It took a few minutes to for me realize that someone was knocking at the door. It was Heather.

"Hey Brian, what's up? I saw your lights on so I knew you were back," she said in her cute little accent.

"Yep, what's that?"

I asked about the dish she held in her hand.

"I cooked tonight and since I noticed that you were back I figured I would bring you something to eat and find out about your latest adventures. I also brought a six-pack."

Heather raised her eyebrows and held the six-pack in the air.

We hung out for while, eating and talking about where I had been and what I had seen over the past week. I told her I had friends coming in from home and that we would be going back to France and a few other places. I could tell she wanted to know more about who was coming, but I moved on because I didn't want to discuss Lexie with her. I knew despite her kindness, she had other feelings for me. After the night with Lyn and Zette, she tried her best to conceal them.

Heather told me about some of her family drama that had been getting to her, which was part of the reason for coming over tonight also. She needed to get out of the house and away from the craziness that she was dealing with. Her father was dating a woman that was the same age as her, and even though her parents are no longer together, the situation was driving her mother crazy. Heather's mom blames her for making the introduction since the girl was a former friend of hers. Heather explained to her mom that her father had always been a womanizer, but her mom refused to accept that fact.

This was like some kind of soap opera, and it was too much drama for me to even listen to. I let it distract me from my anticipation until I couldn't take anymore.

I told Heather that I was going to turn in for the night to give her the hint. Either she didn't get the hint or she just didn't want to leave. I tried again, I thanked her for the food and beer and told her I was going to take a shower and that she could let herself out when she was ready. She still didn't move, so I went and jumped in the shower. I thought I heard what sounded like the door.

After a long hot shower, I felt great. I dried myself off and spread lotion all over my body. I've lived alone for years so I no longer bother with pajamas or anything unless it is really cold. When I came out of the bathroom I found Heather still there, sitting in front of the TV eating chips. She looked over at me and her mouth fell open. She stood up in shock as the chips fell to the floor. I was almost as startled and when I saw Heather's face. I wanted to laugh but didn't want to embarrass her. She was frozen with a mixed look of shock, embarrassment and a sense of thrill at the sight of my naked body. I was enjoying it. Although she had seen my parts before, the situation was entirely different and I don't think she paid much attention to the package. Heather came to and realized she was staring right at my man. She shook her head, and then tried to look away and find something else to focus on while she stammered to get up. I assumed that now she was definitely leaving. I just stood there watching her fumble around. It sounded like she was saying 'see you later' as she rambled. Heading for the door, she looked back and glanced down again at my man. I flexed my pelvic muscles to make my man wave goodnight. Heather jumped, shook her head, and made a little noise that sounded like "oh" as she raced towards the door.

"Heather, wait!"

She seemed nervous as she slowly turned towards me. I walked to her and took her hand in mine. I figured what better way to distract myself from the anticipation of Lexie's arrival than with a romp in the hay with Heather. I touched her face and felt her muscles relax. She closed her eyes and we kissed. Heather let herself go completely and our bodies co-mingled right there on the living room floor for the next two hours. There's nothing like good sex to calm you and make you sleep like a baby. Now I was really ready for Lexie.

Lexie   CHAPTER 17

I couldn't believe that I was on my way to Europe on such short notice. I also couldn't believe that I was unemployed. I didn't know how to deal with that. I kept thinking, 'how am I to respond to people when they ask what I do for a living?' I have never been without a job since I was 16 years old. Now, at thirty, I was getting an idea of what it felt like to be unemployed. Even though it wasn't my fault and the economy was in a state of depression, I still felt a sense of failure that I couldn't shake. I had to constantly remind myself not to take this personally. I had come a long way and had always done a great job. Before the cutbacks, I had all the executives singing my praises. This trip was just what I needed. I couldn't wait to get to London.

I know I said I wouldn't create major damage when I went out on my shopping spree but this was special. It's not every day I get a chance to leave the country on a moment's notice for a romantic excursion. I have to admit, Brooke was no help. Everywhere she turned there was a garment of clothing, a piece of lingerie or a "cute outfit" that I just could not leave the store without. I was only going for a week but you would have thought I was leaving for a month. I could be bad all by myself; Brooke just made the situation worse. But, we did enjoy ourselves and it gave us an opportunity to spend some girlfriend time together before my trip. Besides, if I was going to seal the deal and do this right, I needed all the right items. Everything that I packed was brand new and less than twenty-four hours old: bras, panties, sexy pajamas and cute little numbers that showed off my figure. I was sure not to forget essentials like massage oils and scented candles to set the mood right. To top it all off, I had a new, enhanced figure thanks to David. I was ready for this trip and my wardrobe was screaming, "I am diva, hear me roar!" I was going to show Brian just what he had been missing. I intended to help him make this trip unforgettable.

Over the PA system I could hear the flight attendant announcing that my flight was now boarding first class. I managed to get first class tickets for two reasons. One, coach was sold out and two, I had accumulated quite a few frequent flyer miles during my directorship at Comtel. I was going in style. I paid for my drink and gave the cute bar tender a nice little tip. I am sure he appreciated the tip, but his interest was obviously focused on the gentleman across the bar from me. I thought to myself, gay is playing a close second to jail when you consider where the brothers are.

Feeling pretty, I pranced my sassy behind over towards the check-in area. As I drew near, a really good looking and distinguished gentlemen was approaching. Just as a young, female flight attendant was about to take his first class boarding pass, a fabulous young brother came running out of nowhere. His jet-black, finger-waved hair shined like the stars in the night.

"He's mine baby, that one is mine!" Boy Fabulous screamed. In one swooping motion he grabbed the pass, checked the gentlemen in and delicately placed the boarding pass back into the man's hand, all with the grace of an Alvin Ailey dancer. The man snatched his hand from him and turned in disgust to board his flight.

"You have a good flight now you hear?" the young man chimed, and then let his eyes roll up while he gave his heart two taps.

As I approached him and handed him my first class ticket, he looked at me from head to toe and gave me an approving "you go girl" look and sealed it with a wink and a snap. I smiled, winked and snapped right back at him.

"You go ahead Ms. Thing," he said to me and smiled as I approached the jet way.

Then he let out a hearty laugh. I knew right then and there that this would be one heck of a flight. In fact, I couldn't tell what the flight was like. After the few glasses of wine in the airport and the glass of champagne I had in my first class seat, I was asleep before the plane taxied to the end of the runway. Before I knew it, the pilot was announcing our descent into London's Heathrow Airport.

I jumped up to go to the cramped little airplane restroom to freshen up before seeing Brian. I didn't want to greet him without being totally fresh. I brushed my teeth, washed my mouth out with my travel-sized Listerine and freshened up my face with one of my Neutrogena face cloths. I loved those things. All you needed was a little water and voila!—you had instant lather and a fresh new face. I touched up my hair with my fingers, dabbed on a little face lotion, mascara and some Lip Glass from MAC. I guess I was taking a little too long in the bathroom because Boy Fabulous was knocking on the restroom door.

"Come on Honey, Don't leave us Divas hanging girl," he said.

"I'm coming out now," I shouted through the door.

I took one last glance in the mirror and was pleased. I squirted a hint of Escada and made my way out of the restroom.

"Now I know you ain't go through all that trouble for just anybody. He must be fine," he said.

I smiled at the thought of how Brian would look at me once I got off this plane. Then I realized that I had just spent all that time in the nasty little toilet bin and never relieved the pressure building on my bladder. I spun right back around and ran back in before Boy Fabulous could make his move.

"Girlfriend, no you didn't!" Boy Fabulous said, shocked.

"Sorry, sugar, I'll only be a minute."

I could hear him suck his teeth through the door. I was almost scared to come out because I didn't want him to embarrass me. I handled my business quickly, washed my hands, and came out. Boy Fabulous was standing right outside the door with his hands on his hips starring me right in the face.

"Well how do I look?" I asked him, trying to hold in my laugh.

"Girl, good, now move so I can handle my business. You think you the only one with a man waiting?" he said and let out another hearty laugh.

I made my way to my seat anticipating a smooth landing right in to the arms of my new man.

Brian   CHAPTER 18

I called Lori to see what was up to and ask her for some advice on what I should do to show Lexie a warm welcome. She gave me a few ideas according to what women like. I wanted Lexie to feel good about coming out here and show her a nice time. I arranged for a limo, furnished with a dozen white roses and a bottle of French Chardonnay and a card that stated a few simple instructions. I booked a suite at the Euston Plaza Hotel, a posh and popular hotel in central London, just a few minutes from the theater district.

Lexie's flight was supposed to arrive at about nine in the morning. I had a little time left before her arrival. I brought a half dozen of pink roses with me to place strategically around the hotel suite. I knew Lexie was going to eat this up. In fact, I impressed myself. Assuming that Lexie would want to freshen up as soon as she arrived, I filled the whirlpool tub with a sweet smelling bubble bath and placed some of the pink rose petals in the water on top of the bubbles, around the tub and prepared a delicate path of petals leading from the door to the tub. I stopped for a second to admire my work.

I strategically placed more petals throughout the bedroom and left a single rose lying across the massive king-size bed. I had already ordered a breakfast spread from room service but requested that they hold the order until I called them back. The breakfast and the bath were just the beginning. We had a full day in store: sightseeing, theater and dinner—the works. I knew that Lexie would be pleasantly surprised.

The one thing I forgot was a fresh pair of drawers. I always try to have a crisp, new pair of boxers for times like these but with all the rushing this morning I hadn't bothered to pack any. In fact, I couldn't remember if I had any new ones at the studio. I decided to buy a pair from the boutique inside the hotel's lobby.

When I got to the boutique, all they had are designer labels starting at a minimum of twenty-six pounds—the equivalent of fifty U.S. dollars. Left with no option, I went for one of the less expensive pairs—not a package—but a single pair for around fifty U.S. dollars. I told the clerk to charge it to my room. Those damn drawers had better outlast every pair in my wardrobe. I was going to make sure I wore those expensive boxers every chance I got. I named them my "dress up drawls." Better believe that every time I have to get dressed up for the next year I will be sure to wear them.

As I was rushing out of the boutique, I spotted Heather. That was the last person I wanted to see just before a rendezvous with Lexie. Apparently she worked at the hotel, and it looked as though she was showing a group of visitors the hotel facilities. Instead of heading through the lobby to catch the elevators, I raced for the stairs and took them all the way to the fourth floor. I was hoping she didn't spot me. What kind of luck do I have? My time was running out. I decided not to think about Heather potentially adding any unnecessary drama to the equation, but you never knew with women. Besides, after our little romp in the hay the night before, I thought she was never going to leave.

I glanced at the clock and it was just about time for Lexie to arrive and I was just about ready to receive her.

Lexie　　　　　　　　CHAPTER 19

I couldn't wait to see Brian's handsome chocolate brown face. The people in the airport must have thought I was some type of nut. I raced through the gate, stretching my neck, searching high and low for Brian. I didn't see him anywhere. I even walked back towards the gate before heading to the baggage claim area to make sure I didn't miss him. I felt a pang of disappointment and touch of fear. I began to think that maybe he overslept. I knew he couldn't have forgotten. I had just spoken to him when I left for the airport. I was getting antsy. I was in a foreign country and that man was nowhere to be found.

I calmed myself down and thought that he was probably waiting for me in the baggage area even though I really wanted him to meet me at the gate. After releasing a huge exasperated gasp of air, I turned to see a stout gentleman wearing a top hat and a black tux. I started to laugh when I realized he was holding a sign with my last name on it. With that I blushed, and all of the excitement and nervous energy came rushing back. I couldn't believe Brian sent a limo for me. I assumed he was waiting outside in the limo.

I raised my hand for the stout driver to notice me and walked to where he was standing.

"Good morning, Ms. Mitchell. I am your driver, Simon—welcome to London," he said in a cute little British accent

"Oh could you say that again? I loved the sound of it," I asked and giggled.

At first he just stared at me as if he didn't understand, then smiled and repeated his greeting. Tickled pink and filled with excitement I laughed and politely returned his greeting.

"Your luggage should be right this way Ma'am," Simon said.

"Why thank you Simon," I said in my own mockery of a British accent. "Just don't call me Ma'am anymore, feel free to call me 'Lexie.'"

Simon smiled and agreed.

The stretch limo was fabulous. I was in heaven. I couldn't wait to see Brian and thank him for the wonderful welcome. I almost opened the limo door myself. Little Mr. Simon came running his stiff, pudgy body towards me to open the door for me before I could get in.

"Don't worry, Simon. You don't have to make a fuss over me." I didn't know what was wrong with me but all of my etiquette went out the window and I didn't care. I had to remind myself that it was okay to be pampered. My main focus was getting my hands on Brian.

I let out a giggle-scream when I looked into the car and found a dozen of roses, a bottle of wine and a card from Brian. I finally figured out this was a little game he was playing and I was ready for whatever came next. The card was actually a note stating that there was a change of plans and that I was on my way to the Euston Plaza Hotel to begin a day of adventure. I just could not stop giggling and thought, 'I think I love him already.' I sat back, smelled the roses and enjoyed the ride.

The hotel was exquisite. I approached the front desk and gave my name and was given a key to my room. The attendant said that my bags would be up shortly and told me to enjoy my stay. As I turned I finally observed the lobby, which was decorated with English elegance but wasn't too overdone. By this time my cheeks were hurting from smiling and blushing. I felt like I was living a dream. Brian was scoring some big time points. I couldn't wait to see what he had in store. I found my way to my room way down towards the end of the hall and I realized it was a suite.

There I stood trying not to jump up and down like a little girl. This time I muffled my scream. I didn't want anyone to hear me, especially Brian. I put my key in the door and reminded myself that a diva can't act like she is not used to things—that's a direct violation of the 'diva code.' I opened the door and couldn't believe my eyes. The suite was incredible. It looked like a luxury apartment from Park Avenue. The entrance led to a grand foyer with a large, round, mahogany console that was adorned with a beautifully hand-painted vase filled with fresh, exotic flowers. As I walked further into the suite I fixed my eyes on an elegantly furnished living room with a wet bar, a formal dining area and a beautiful, black baby-grand piano perched on a platform, looking out on gigantic floor-to-ceiling windows. I called out to Brian, but there was no answer. I decided to check out the rest of the suite. There was a small powder room near the entrance adorned with terracotta colored marble walls and countertops, and ornate chrome fixtures. I walked further to find the bedroom, which was decorated in typical hotel fashions. Some interior designer got paid big bucks to decorate this room with loud matching patterns for the carpet, bedding and window treatments. I blushed when I saw rose petals spread around the room and a beautiful single rose lying across the massive king-size bed. There was a door across the room, which I assumed was either a closet or master bathroom. I gently pushed open the door, taking in the incredible view of the huge, full black and white marble bathroom, including a sauna. To my pleasant surprise, there were more rose petals spread across the floor. There was an amazing fragrance wafting though the air. I closed my eyes to take it in and felt a presence before me.

A little startled I opened my eyes to see Brian standing right in front of me, so close I could feel his breath. At that very moment Brian looked as delectable as a box of Godiva chocolates. I wanted to take a bite out of him. My purse, the hotel keycard, and my sweater dropped to the floor so that I could grab my man and show him just how much I appreciated everything he had done to welcome me. Brian and I kissed a long sensuous kiss, so long that we had to stop to catch our breath. There we stood staring at each other, panting like a pair of wolves in heat. Words weren't necessary. I felt like I was riding on cloud nine. I snapped out of it and screamed.

"Brian, I am so happy to see you. You didn't have to do all of that, the limo and all. I thought you were going to meet me at the airport. I was…"

Brian looked at me, rolled his eyes and laughed. I realized I was talking a mile a minute so I shut up right in the middle of my sentence.

Brian placed his index finger across my lips. Without breaking the romantic silence, he slowly undressed me. I was a little embarrassed when he got to my bra because my headlights were now on full blast from the simple touch of his hands and the sweet, masculine scent of his well-toned body. Brian led me to the steamy whirlpool filled with bubbles and decorated with pretty pink rose petals. I began to blush. My cheeks felt like they were now on fire. I stepped in, closed my eyes and slid down into the warmth allowing the fragrance, water and ambiance to overcome me. Brian left me alone to soak.

After what felt like hours, I emerged from the bath, oiled my body with sweet body oil. I blow-dried and flat ironed my frizzy hair courtesy of the exotic steamy bathroom. I slipped on a cute, little bronze colored dress that Brooke picked out for me from BCBG and went searching for Brian. As I approached the living room I heard the mellow sounds of Maxwell floating softly through the air. Brian was standing near the dining table over an immaculate spread.

"I didn't know what you wanted so I took the liberty of ordering everything on the menu," Brian said.

Immediately after that stolen line from Richard Gere in the film Pretty Woman, Brian and I both burst out laughing.

"It was smooth, right? Tell me it wasn't smooth," Brian said, still laughing. I was bent over holding my stomach.

"Did I ever tell you, you need to take your show on the road? No more Brian, please, no more. And don't quit your day job."

"Come on, Lexie, tell me that wasn't funny."

"It was hilarious, but right now, my mind is on food. I could eat a horse," I said, eyeing the delectable spread.

Brian wasn't lying, he did order everything on the menu or at least it seemed like he did. There were eggs, bacon, pancakes, croissants, ice-cold sparkling water, freshly squeezed orange juice, bagels with a choice of whipped butter in the shape of doves and an assortment of flavored whipped cream cheeses. He even ordered a number of breakfast cereals. I couldn't believe my eyes and certainly couldn't eat all that was there.

It was a great day indeed, and it had only just begun. By the time the day was done, I had seen all that London had to offer, from Big Ben to the Queen's quarters. We saw a marvelous play down in the theater district and dined at an elegant establishment with appetizing seafood dishes. When the evening wound down, I was completely exhausted—but not too exhausted to show Brian how much of a good time I had by ending the night with a bang!

When Brian and I got back to the suite, we hurriedly undressed with the intensity of the famous love scenes from the movie Fatal Attraction. Lips locked, we managed to remove all of our garments, making our way to the king-sized love nest. Brian swept me off of my feet and carried me up the two steps leading to the massive bed. Nearly dropping me, Brian covered my naked body with his. Still kissing, Brian inserted his fingers into my womanhood to gage the consistency. Brian entered me with purpose, holding me tight as he drove his manhood into me wholeheartedly.

Brian stopped right in the middle of a down stroke and proceeded to cover my middle with his warm lips. My back arched involuntarily and I released moans of pleasure. Taking all of me in, he toyed with me until I was ready to burst. Lapping at the steady flow of juices, Brian inserted his fingers into my vagina. Pumping and licking until he sent me into an erotic frenzy. My body racked with pleasure, sending spasms to the end of my being.

The tables turned and it was my turn to pleasure him. Matching the passion that had sparked this exhilarating love session, I turned him on his back, stood over him, and lowered myself onto his nature. We rode together until we reached our pleasure peaks. I collapsed on top of him and we fell into a restful slumber.

The next morning the gig was up. We checked out of the posh hotel and headed over to Brian's rented studio to prepare for a regular night on the town and pack up for our train ride to the next stop on this journey: Paris.

Brian   CHAPTER 20

I enjoyed Lexie's company in London. Although the remainder of
our vacation won't be as elaborate as the first day, we certainly have
our plates full. I was happy I managed to avoid running into
Heather when we left the hotel. I checked out through the express
system so that I didn't have to chance seeing her in the lobby. The
bellboy came right to our room and took our bags to the awaiting
taxi. We came back to my studio and collapsed again for a few more
hours of rest. It was time to get ready for part two: Paris. Our train
would be leaving in a couple of hours. I wanted to get a good workout in before we headed out, so I let Lexie sleep. She was intoxicated from the drinks and sexual escapade from the previous night.
I didn't think she would be interested in getting up at the crack of
dawn to work out.

Just as my workout was getting good, I heard Lexie awaken.
Even though she looked a mess and was obviously hung over, she
was still a fine lady. She looked cute in my T-shirt. Lexie watched me
doing calisthenics and pulled the covers over her mouth.

"Good morning," she mumbled, then got up and raced to the
bathroom to freshen up.

When she returned, she looked a bit tamer. She gracefully
walked towards me with her lips puckered, ready to give me a big
kiss then stopped dead in her tracks. She placed her hand over her

mouth as if she was about to throw up last night's dinner.

"Oh Brian, is that you or did you sauté some onions for breakfast?" she teased and let out a hearty cry of laughter.

I had to laugh too. I had been working for about an hour and the studio did smell like a gym locker after a wrestling match.

"I was just kidding baby, I like your man-funk," Lexie said reaching for me.

After that comment I grabbed her, placed her head right in the pit of my underarm and held her tight so she couldn't break loose.

"Ha, there you go," I teased.

I quickly let her go and raced for the bathroom before she could find something to throw at me.

"Yuck, Brian. You are so disgusting!" she screamed as she tossed pillows and anything else within her reached towards me.

I had fun with Lexie and I realized that simple fun was what was missing from all of my previous relationships. Even with Lori. We were real cool, but never had this much fun together. When Lexie and I were together, anything could be made into a joke that we could elaborate on for hours.

While I was in the shower, Lexie opened the bathroom door to tell me that she was making breakfast and asked if I had any special requests. I told her yes, collard greens, macaroni and cheese and some fried chicken. She just slammed the door shut without even responding. A second later I heard the door creak open. Lexie flushed the toilette and ran out, causing my shower water to run cold. I knew she was on the other side of the door laughing and waiting to hear me yell. I refused to give her the satisfaction.

As I was drying off, I heard the bell ring. At first I panicked because I knew it couldn't be anyone but Heather. Lexie yelled from the kitchen to ask if I wanted her to get it. I appreciated that fact that she asked instead of just taking her nosy ass to my door. I also assumed this was a test to see what I would say. I was still wet and naked. I yelled out to her that I would be right out.

I wrapped my towel around my waist and headed for the door. I guess Lexie didn't hear my response over the Jill Scott's cut flowing throughout the studio. She was on her way to the door. Please don't let this be Heather. Please be the mail man or someone else. I sped up to try to get to the door before Lexie without being obvious.

"Who is it?" she yelled and was about to turn the knob.

"You got my greens going girl?" I said, smacking her behind. I attempted to reach the door knob before she did.

She playfully slapped me on the butt with the kitchen towel and opened the door. There stood Heather dressed in work clothes, staring at Lexie as if she had two heads. Lexie said 'hello' but apparently Heather failed to hear her. Lexie repeated herself, this time in a rather indignant tone. I quickly stepped forward to greet Heather and redirect both of their attention before some female shit jumped off. Heather's gaze was fixated on Lexie and she still had not responded.

"What the hell is her problem?" Lexie said and turned to me with her finger nearly touching Heather's nose.

"Can you hear, miss?" Lexie said to Heather.

I leaped between the two women and called Heather's name. Heather snapped out of her daze then finally looked at me.

"Excuse me," She finally said to Lexie.

"Hey Heather, what's up?" I asked.

Lexie waved her hand in the air, started mumbling something, and went back into the kitchen.

"Oh I am sorry, I didn't realize you had company," Heather said, looking uneasy.

"Yeah that's my girl Lexie from home. What's up?" I asked.

Heather's eyes stretched at the word "girl." I know I overstated the situation, but I knew it was the safest thing to do. Lexie was hanging on every word. I had nothing to loose when it came to Heather. Still, I didn't want to be disrespectful, nor did I want a scene. I also didn't want Lexie to sense that Heather and I were involved in any way. I was confident that I had made Lexie comfortable enough so that I wouldn't have to deal with this for the rest of our vacation.

Heather couldn't seem to think of what she wanted.

"Oh I just realized that you were back and I just stopped by to say hello and see what was up but I see that you're busy," she said and looked down at the towel around my waist.

"Oh yeah, well I'm cool. I'm about to head out again, you know. We'll be back in a couple of days. I'll catch up with you then."

"Sure," Heather said awkwardly, "have fun."

She looked disappointed and turned to leave.

I said a quick thank you to God as I closed the door. Lexie was still mumbling under her breath while she continued breakfast.

"Is that the one keeping you tuned up over here?" she asked.

She totally caught me off guard with that question.

I tried to play it off and realized that Lexie is a smarter one. I left that one alone and simply didn't respond.

"Don't worry, I understand folks need maintenance. But I'm here now so girlfriend has to rely on self service," Lexie commented and laughed.

She ran over to me and jumped on my back then started planting sweet gentle kisses over the top of my head. I liked her even more, but she also had me worried. For the first time I wondered who was keeping her tuned up while I was away, and I didn't like the idea one bit.

Lexie   CHAPTER 21

I had the time of my life. London, France and Florence all wrapped up in one vacation. This was one vacation I would never forget, especially that little visit from the tune-up woman, Heddy, or whatever her name is. I wasn't mad. I couldn't expect him to hang out dry for three months waiting on me. Besides, he was sure to let me know that I should have all the fun I could during his absence. Should I not expect him to have his?

I was very thankful to Brian for the experience and tried my best to show him just how thankful I was, over and over again. Now it was back to reality. I was on my way back to New York. Brooke was picking me up at the airport. I knew she was going to want to hear it all. I hadn't spoken to her since my departure ten days ago. I originally planned to come back after only a week, but Brian and I were having such a good time that I changed my return flight and stayed a few extra days. Everything about the trip was great: the sightseeing, the food and most of all Brian.

The blasted pilot spoke a little too loudly into the PA system. He apparently startled quite a few sleeping passengers as he announced our decent into JFK International Airport. Although I had a ball, I was glad to be home. I did have some mixed feelings. I thought to myself, what was I coming home to? I have no job!

Maybe it was time for me to start my own business. But what would I do? I didn't have the energy to think about this now. These thoughts were starting to depress me. I redirected my thoughts to what would happen when Brian returned home. He had little over a week left before he was to come home, which meant I had a little time to have all the single fun I could have. If this thing worked out with Brian, I wanted to be sure to have no regrets. If it didn't, I needed a backup plan. The clock is ticking and I need to get a move on when it comes to a solid relationship with the potential for marriage. But marriage didn't really have a stronghold on me. I almost didn't care if I ever got married. I just didn't want to feel lonely.

As the airplane's wheels hit the ground with a thud, reality settled in. The additional bags I acquired from my trip, symbolized the weight of decisions to come. Adjusting to life after the layoff will be a challenge. I gathered all of my things and trudged along until I finally reached the baggage claim area. The idea of being home was not as comforting as it had always been for me.

"LEXIE!" Brooke came running towards me.

The guard stopped her at the gate. I started to go over to her assuming since she didn't have a claim ticket she wouldn't be able to get past the guard. Then again, this was Brooke we were talking about. Brooke had the gift of gab and could talk her way in or out of any situation. Before I knew it, Brooke was on the inside approaching my way fast. I looked back towards the guard who was now wearing a wide clumsy smile. I said to myself, "If he only knew."

"Lexie you have to tell me everything!" We hugged and before I could respond Brooke interrupted, "Start from the beginning! I can't wait to hear the whole story...wait, don't start now. Let's go to breakfast and we can discuss the whole thing over pancakes!"

Finally after catching her breath and realizing that I had yet to speak, Brooke looked me over and smiled.

"What?" I asked.

"I know I was going a mile a minute, but I am glad you are back." Brooke stared at me with a wicked smile. "What I wouldn't pay to be in your shoes right now."

We laughed, hugged and rocked from side to side.

The loud buzz broke our embrace indicating the highly antic-ipated arrival of my luggage.

"Brooke, I brought you back something," I said. Brooke's eyes grew wide with excitement

"You did! You didn't have to do that. But I am glad you did."

"You know I had to bring something back for my girl. You are going to love it."

"What is it, already?" she whined. I enjoyed teasing her.

"You'll have to wait." Brooke rolled her eyes but the big smile remained.

We climbed into Brooke's black BMW X5 in search of the nearest IHOP. I suddenly had a craving for pecan pancakes and hot cocoa with whipped cream on the top. We jumped on the Belt Parkway heading towards the IHOP on Sunrise Highway. Suddenly an uneasy feeling came over me, and I turned towards Brooke.

"BROOKE!" I screamed and pointed to an oversized SUV headed our way.

Brooked turned immediately and made every attempt to avoid the fate that was inevitably heading our way. She sped up then slowed down while trying to maneuver out of the way of the oncom-ing truck. The only thing on the other side of us was cement, grass, and trees. It seemed like minutes, but it all happened in a matter of seconds.

BOOM! We felt the impact of the truck slamming into us. We spun around at least twice, bounced off of the cement overpass before a tree finally broke our momentum. I reached out for Brooke. I felt her but couldn't speak. Brooke didn't respond at all. The silence was deafening. The colors before me began to fade and blend together before total darkness took over. Everything faded into blackness.

Brian   CHAPTER 22

With Lexie gone, I was ready to go home. I had seen all I really wanted to see and felt that there was nothing left for me in Europe. Although I only had another couple of days before my trip ended, I decided it was time to go home and get back to my real life. Besides, the holiday season would be rolling around shortly and I wanted...actually I needed to be around my own people.

It had only been a day since Lexie had gone back home and I wanted to see her. I hadn't heard from her since her return and thought that was a little peculiar. I tried to reach her several times only to get her machine. I didn't want to leave too many messages because I didn't want her to think that I was sweating her. Not hearing from her at all made me want to hop on the next flight out and hunt her down. She was in my system.

It was time to handle my business with her and seal the fate of the sorry ass that had been keeping her tuned up in my absence. I couldn't put my finger on it, but I felt that her presence was calling me back home and I couldn't wait to get there.

After adjusting all of my travel arrangements, I found that I was able to head home a few days earlier. I paid my rent up to my original departure date so I knew I wouldn't have a problem with the landlord. I figured I should make the best of my remaining few days. This was the first time since I had arrived in Europe that I didn't have any real plans. I figured I would check Heather and the girls and say goodbye to them. They were great hostesses. Tony the Tiger grrrreat!

I was checking out the local movie listings when someone started knocking on my door like they wanted to take it of the hinges. I heard Heather's voice on the other side screeching.

"Brian, please... open the door. I need your help!" she panted.

"What the...?" was all I could muster.

I got up and swung the door open. I braced myself for the drama that I assumed was to follow. Heather stood in the archway looking weary. I wasn't sure if she was mad at someone or had just been attacked on the street.

"What's up with you?" I wasn't being very polite but I really didn't feel like being bothered at this particular time and wanted her to know it.

"Brian," Heather crooned in her sweet British accent.

I felt myself soften while my man hardened. I become aroused at the oddest moments. Here Heather was standing in my doorway looking wild and teary eyed as if she had been mugged or lost a fight with a pit bull, and the whole scene was turning me on.

Heather's babbling snapped me out of my daydream of us romping in the clothes piled up on the bed that still needed to be packed.

"I'm sorry Heather, what's going on?"

"Oh my goodness, Brian, you didn't hear a word I said, did you?"

Heather looked like she was going to start wailing any minute. I gave her my undivided attention.

"Come in." I stepped out of the way to let her in and closed the door. "Now, slow down and tell me what's wrong, you were rambling and I could hardly understand a word you said." I lied.

Heather cupped the crown of her head with her hands and started pacing quickly back and forth.

"That bastard," she spat through clenched teeth while I watched her nipples bounce around under her baby tee.

"What bastard Heath? What's up?"

"My sister's boyfriend beat her up bad."

"What do you mean?"

As if 'beat her up bad' gave way to infinite possibilities. I let that dumb question slide. Apparently so did Heather.

"She's at my apartment right now. He beat her up. She's all bruised up and has a black eye. She came straight to my house for help. I can't believe that bastard," she huffed.

"Heather, what do you need me to do?"

I was hoping she wouldn't say go after him because first of all, I don't do domestic disputes and secondly, the last thing I need is to get into something just before I head home. With my luck, my ass would be sitting up in some British bull pen somewhere defending myself against some ignorant British thugs.

"I am so sorry, Brian, I didn't want to drag you into this but I was so upset when she came to my house, I just didn't know what to do. The first thing I thought was to come over here and get you to help us out. I realize that's not the best idea. If you can just come over to my place and hang out with us while I try to convince her to go to the authorities that would be fine."

"Why, are you afraid he's going to come by?" I asked, so that I'd know if I should be prepared for anything crazy.

"Yes, would you please just come by? If he comes and find another man there then he won't try anything," Heather pleaded.

"All right, let me get my sneakers, I'll go back with you now."

"Thanks, Brian, I really appreciate this. I promise this won't be a big issue."

I sat on the couch to get my sneakers on and thought about not bothering. I was not in the mood for this although I didn't want anything to happen to Heather or her sister, especially if it could be avoided.

"Have your sister and her man been together long?"

"Seven years."

Heather rolled her eyes when she answered.

"I take it you don't like him too much."

"Hate him!" She said with contempt.

"Do they fight often?"

"Often enough. She's kicks him out, but keeps letting him come back."

"Damn!"

I finished tying my sneaker, jumped up from the couch and reached for my hooded sweatshirt.

"All right, Heather, let's go."

"Thanks again, Brian I know his crippled behind won't try anything with you around."

"Crippled? What do you mean crippled?"

"Heather said, "He has problems with one of his knees and walks with a cane. He was in a really bad biking accident and it also damaged his eye sight. He's legally blind in one eye."

Now I was stupefied and couldn't believe my ears.

"Heather, you mean to tell me your sister got her ass beat by a brother who can barely walk straight, and can only see out of one eye?"

"Yes, Brian!" Heather let out a huge sigh.

I tried my best to suppress the laugh that was applying pressure on my ribs.

"Wait, so you are saying that he gave her a black eye with a bum leg and one good eye?

"Yes Brian!" Heather said and sighed again.

I lost it. I laughed so hard I gave myself a migraine. After about ten minutes, Heather came to pick me up off the floor and dragged me through the door kicking and laughing. By that time I had blinded myself with tears. I gained some composure and stopped.

"What's this really about Heather?" I asked.

"Why would you ask that?" she questioned and looked away.

"What would make you come to me for this and not someone in your family who knows him, like your father?

Heather looked as though she was getting frustrated. I couldn't help but feel like there were alterior motives involved here.

"I just wanted you to come. Please! I'll make it up to you before you leave."

"Fine. Let's go."

We checked up on Heather's sister who seemed to be doing fine. She did appear a little scuffed but seemed to be okay. Heather and I went to grab a bite to eat and ended up back at my place in the bed.

Chapter 23

Lexie

I attempted to open my eyes and was nearly blinded by stark, fluorescent lighting. It took several minutes to gain my composure and realize I was lying in a hospital bed. The pounding in my head became much more pronounced as I tried to focus on the setting. The bright lights forced me to shut my eyes immediately without fully taking in my surroundings. Then I did the worst thing I could do, I shook my head in a failed attempt to gather my composure. Internal hammering engulfed me. I tried to massage my temple only to disperse more pain throughout every nerve in my body. My left temple was soft. Fear cradled me. Fresh tears stung my eyes as I tried to put together the elements of my circumstance.

A strong male presence held my hand in his while gently rubbing my hair making my tears stream more steadily. I was rocking from side to side as my entire body quaked.

"It will be all right," a deep soothing voice softly whispered.

"Brian," I managed to whimper. It hurt to speak, which made me cry harder. I heard a sigh and felt the strong hands holding my soul together fall away. I strained to open my eyes. Curiosity had the best of me. Who was this man? Finally gaining focus, my eyes carved out David's frame standing beside me.

"It's okay," David said as he took my hands in his and touched the side of my face.

Wiping my eyes as well as the mucus above my lip sent a new stroke of pain to the back of my hand where the IV had been inserted. I managed to speak again through the tears.

"I'm sorry David."

"No problem, I understand. I just wanted to be here when you opened your eyes. I am going to go and call your parents and your sisters and let them know you're awake."

"David, wait!"

I whimpered and tried to reach for him. Pain struck the hand with the IV once again. I moaned.

"Yes, Lexie."

David diverted his eyes from me and hung his head.

"Uh, how long have I been asleep?" I muttered, grimacing from the pain again.

I was afraid to hear the answer.

"Since the accident yesterday morning," David said. He seemed jittery."

My heart dropped, I couldn't believe that much time had passed. An entire day of my life lost. And then it hit me—accident. David said I was in an accident.

"Look Lexie, I need... I'm going to run call your family and let the doctor know that you are awake now, okay? I will be right back."

"David, wait! What happened?"

David turned his back on me and dropped his head into his hands. I sprang up, casting spasms of pain through my body. David looked to the ceiling fluttering his eyes.

"David...Oh my God! Please, tell me what happened to me."

Then I remembered Brooke.

"Where's Brooke?"

Slowly turning to face me, David sighed again.

"I'll be right back," he said and quickly turned and sped out of the room.

The throbbing forced away my thoughts. I looked around at all of the machines making noises around me. I had tubes in my nose, an IV in the back of my hand and a cast on my right leg and right pinky finger. I stared at my hands for minutes, taking in the bruises along both arms. I lifted my hand to my face only to spark a new series of aches. Carefully, I explored my face with both hands, finding tender swollen eyes, cheeks and temples. I could only image what I must have looked like. I began to weep again into my aching hands.

The beeping sounds from the nearby machines kept intruding my unclear thoughts, adding to the present state of confusion. I wanted to throw something at the machines to shut them up but could barely find the strength to even lift my hands, much less lift something to throw. Slowly I laid back and focused on the sounds of the television over my head, hoping it would drown out the constant beeping. I needed to know what happened to me and it pained me ever more not being able to recall the events that caused me to cast a precious day of my life into the unknown.

Just when I began to think about how lonely I felt, David reentered the room. He told me that he called my mother to let her know that I was awake and that my family was on their way here. David stood over me, taking in all of my injuries. It was then that I remembered the tender side of him, the same David that I once loved. The David that a certain part of me would always love. Before

I could say a word, he began to pour his heart out to me.

"Lexie, I know you may not want to hear this, and this may not even be the right time, but I have to say it. To me there is no better time than the present." I braced myself as David continued. "Lexie, I realize that I did you wrong."

"David, it doesn't..."

I tried to stop him with a weak wave of my hand to let him know that he didn't need to go there.

"Lexie it does matter," David interrupted. "Yes, it has been a long time. But I still love you. I know I was wrong. But since you have been out of my life, it hasn't been the same. I never got a chance to explain myself—I know you will say there is nothing to explain. I needed to let you know that no matter what I can't loose you. When I heard about your accident, I was the first one here and stayed until I saw you open your eyes. The thought of losing you all over again made me crazy. So I can't afford to pass up on taking this chance. You need somebody now and I want to be there for you. We can take it slow, Lexie. You can trust me again. I am sure of it."

I couldn't control the tears that flowed from my eyes. I didn't want David to see me affected by his words. I was raw and vulnerable. No matter how hard I tried, I couldn't shield the fact that his words had touched me, yet I still couldn't say that it was what I wanted and I didn't have the strength to oppose. I closed my eyes and saw Brian's face. I felt David's lips lightly brush my forehead and he was gone. I became angry. How could he do this to me? Why now? Hadn't I had enough blows for one lifetime?

Brian   CHAPTER 2 4

I still hadn't heard from Lexie and admittedly I was disappointed. I was determined to get back home.

Heather and I were due to have breakfast and she would then carry me and what remained of my belongings to the airport. Heather tried to avoid me after the incident with her sister. It's still funny to me how we ended up in bed that night. I knew there was a motive. She came over last night for a few farewell cocktails. Initially she was a little uneasy, but she quickly loosened up after a few sips of her favorite Russian Vodka. By the end of the night, we shared a lot more than cocktails. That's when she offered to take me to the airport. In return I decided to treat her to breakfast to show my appreciation.

Heather arrived looking quite sexy. I knew she had gone all out for me since this would be our last time seeing one another for a long time—possibly forever. Heather donned a nicely-fitted black skirt and a tight, lavender, buttoned-down shirt with only the two buttons near her breast closed. She wore silky, black stockings and a pair of "screw-me-now-stilettos."

"All this for breakfast? Wow!" I teased.

Heather flashed a suggestive smile and I wondered if the place we were going to for breakfast had poles. I pondered the possibilities of skipping breakfast, going straight to dessert and then the airport. I pushed the thoughts from my mind and proceeded with our original plans. I knew exactly what Heather was doing and I must admit it was working on me.

We vowed to stay in touch even though I knew then I probably wouldn't. Although Heather was really a nice person, once I set foot in the homeland, my focus would be on Lexie.

Breakfast was great and Heather even shed a few tears. A part of me would surely miss her. I thoroughly enjoyed my time away, yet it was time for me to get back to my life. I had a huge agenda to attend to. Besides Lexie, I also had to focus my energies on getting new jobs and finding new clients. I wanted to see my mother's face, hang out with my boys and sleep in my own bed. Jeff offered to pick me up at the airport. I had a long flight ahead of me and plenty on my mind to keep me busy along the way.

139

The flight went quite smoothly or maybe I was so engrossed in my thoughts I didn't notice otherwise. As soon as I approached the baggage claim area I caught sight of Jeff. I retrieved my bags, went over to him and gave my boy a pound and the type of hug men are comfortable giving one another.

"How was your trip?" Jeff asked as we exited the airport. "Man, how many people do I know that can run off and take a trip like you?" he joked.

"I'm just trying to live a little. I must say, it was unreal." I replied, thinking back.

"So what's up with the ladies over there? I know you've got some stories." Jeff paused a moment to imagine the possibilities.

"Well, come to think of it, I got one story you are going to love. You won't believe it," I said thinking about the night with Lynn and Zette.

Jeff and I grabbed my bags and jumped in the car. I proceeded to fill him in on both the adventures and misadventures of my trip, from the threesome to Heather and the brief encounter with Heather and Lexie.

Jeff occasionally interjected with "What?" and "Are you serious man?" Then I filled him in on my game plan with Lexie.

"Lexie's all right, I can see the two of you together. Go for it."

Jeff's face revealed his approval. Suddenly he became quiet and I could tell he was pondering something.

"What's up with you?" I quizzed.

Jeff frowned and slightly shook his head. Then he released a loud sigh.

"What is it?" I blurted impatiently before he could get the first word out.

Jeff sighed again before attempting to speak once more.

"You don't wanna hear this!" Jeff shook his head from side to side again. After a few minutes he finally said. "Shelly is about to have a baby."

I was confused and couldn't understand what that had to do with me. The confusion must have registered all over my face because Jeff looked at me and obviously felt the need to inject a little clarity into my state of bewilderment.

"She said it's yours, man!" he added.

"You can't be serious. That's crazy. I haven't even been here for the past three months. How is she gonna say it's mine?" I couldn't believe my ears. I shook my head and started staring out the window.

"You need to talk to her and get this straight. She came to me with it—just showed up at my house one night with her stomach out to here." Jeff put his hand out a distance from his stomach and continued. "I think she's about to have that baby sometime soon. She came to my house looking for you. She had been trying to get to you but couldn't find you. I just said to her that you were out of town and I wasn't sure when you'd be back. Don't be surprised if she's camped out at your apartment waiting for you to get home. You never know what to expect from her." Jeff nodded again as his face formed a weak smile.

I felt the muscles in my face constrict. If she's that far along then there could very well be a possibility that it could be mine: yet I wasn't convinced. I would certainly get to the bottom of this–and quick. I wasn't looking forward to being a baby's daddy of a deranged woman. The rest of the ride was a blur as my anger festered. By the time Jeff dropped me off, I was seething. Realizing how pissed I was, Jeff told me he would come by later. He helped me get my bags in and abruptly left.

I dropped my bags at the door and headed straight for the phone. I noticed the message indicator on my answering machine blinking and wondered who called, especially when just about everyone knew that I was out of town and wasn't expected to be back for at least a few more days. I quickly scanned through the messages. Shelly had left over fifteen messages. I erased every one of them. I would deal with her soon enough. The last message I listened to said something about Lexie being in a bad accident. I felt a dense thud land in the pit of my stomach. My thoughts were in such disarray that I couldn't fully grasp the particulars of the message. I slammed down the off button, grabbed my keys and headed for the car.

141

Lexie   CHAPTER 2 5

After a few days and a plethora of annoying tests, I was finally released from the hospital. Brooke, on the other hand, had a longer way to go. As a result of the accident she suffered a broken pelvic bone guaranteeing a long road to recovery. I was deeply depressed and I felt responsible for her condition.

Despite Brooke's and everyone else's attempts to convince me that this was not my fault, I felt horrible. If I hadn't asked her to pick me up from the airport the accident would never have happened. I couldn't help but feel guilty for causing so much pain to my best friend. I spent as much time with her in the hospital as I possibly could – doing whatever I could to make her stay more comfortable. I was happy to see that she maintained her spunk.

David had been at my beck and call since the incident, yet my thoughts stayed with Brian. Despite what David had done for me, I realized that I was definitely over him. I wanted to call Brian overseas but didn't want to burden him with my ordeal. The anticipation of expecting him soon was getting the best of me.

My doorbell rang and I rolled my eyes. It took a lot for me to hobble around and I wasn't in the mood for company. I wanted to be left alone to my thoughts about Brian. Mom, Dionne and Ava had just left, so I assumed it had to be David.

"I'm coming," I scowled as I struggled to lift myself from my couch.

The ringing became more intense. It angered me, which caused me to hobble a little bit faster, anxious to see who was at my door. I swung the door open poised to let David have it for being so impatient, instead I set eyes on a ruffled Brian standing in my entry.

I froze. Neither of us made an attempt to close the gap between us. We stood staring each other down.

"Brian," I whispered softly as I covered my trembling lips.

"Lexie, what's up, partner?" he asked and we embraced.

A flood of emotions flowed through me as Brian held me. I hadn't felt this comfortable since the accident.

Brian pulled back from me and looked into my eyes. He examined the slightly healed bruises on my face and fingered them softly. His concentrated gaze brought back the pain and depression. I began to cry. He stared into my eyes, searching for some kind of answer to what he was witnessing. My lips began to tremble more feverishly as the tears flowed. Brian then lifted my chin and gently swept his thumb across my lips to quiet the tremors. He kissed the tears creeping down my face and brought his lips to mine. My lips parted in anticipation. Brian planted several tender kisses before taking me in fully. I wrapped my arms around him and pulled him closer, matching his zeal. My tears cascaded over our entwined lips. The kiss stole my wind, leaving me breathless.

Just then we heard someone clear his throat. Together we turned to see David standing by with bags of what looked like Chinese food and wearing a look mixed with disappointment and anger. He fixed his gaze upon Brian. Brian challenged his glare. I decided it was a good time for me to interject. I cleared my own

143

throat loudly before speaking.

"Hello David. This is Brian, Brian, this is David."

Neither spoke nor acknowledged my weak introduction. I pulled my arms from around Brian.

"Brian, why don't you wait inside for me," I said hoping he would oblige without hesitation.

David and Brian remained locked in their gaze until Brian slowly stepped into the house. I felt bad for David. Yet I wasn't sorry for what he witnessed. He sighed heavily, turning his head sideways.

"So what's up with that Lexie?"

Frustration registered in his brow before he lowered his eyes and voice. I massaged my throbbing temples and closed my eyes to collect my thoughts.

"David, I don't know what you want me to say."

David was seething. He shoved the food he brought into my hands and turned away.

"Whatever Lexie, I'm gone," he said walking off.

He swiftly turned back towards me, snatched the food from my hands, turned on his heels, and said, "He won't eat anything my money bought."

Brian was calling my name from inside the apartment as I stood there replaying the entire scene over in my head. I raised my hands in defeat and headed through my apartment door. Brian was coming from my kitchen as I closed the door behind me. I was so engrossed in seeing him I didn't think to ask what made him come back from Europe early. I was sure with all of my war wounds he was certainly going to be interested in what I had been up to since I left him a few days ago.

I hopped over to the couch and flopped down. At first Brian

just stared at me. I knew he was pondering the David situation and decided to wait and see if he would say anything about it. Just as I thought, he came out with it.

"So, what's the deal with your ex? Has he been the one taking care of you while I've been gone?"

His question made me recall the "friendly" visit from that girl in London.

"No Brian. David has just been looking out for me since my accident. He just came to bring me something to eat. Believe me when I say there is nothing going on there." Then I thought about it for a minute. "What's wrong? Don't tell me you're jealous?"

"I just want to know what's up," he said and smiled.

I caught him.

"Rest assured, there is nothing 'up' between David and I."

"Yeah, all right," he said, not looking convinced.

"You know it's all about you partner," I teased and leaned over to squeeze his cheek.

In the process I turned a little too quickly and groaned from the pain that shot up my injured leg.

"Hey, you better watch that before you break something else," Brian teased.

He got up, went into the kitchen and returned with a steaming cup of tea on a tray and placed it on the coffee table. He then sat on the opposite end of the couch and stared at me. I noticed his gaze as I reached for the teacup. I met his gaze as I sat back and took a sip of the steaming substance.

"Umm, Lemon Zinger, my favorite," I said cuddling into the couch and enjoying the flavor as it danced across my tongue.

"Are you going to tell me about this accident?" he asked.

"Are you going to sit a little closer to me?" I asked and I patted the empty space on the couch beside me.

"I didn't want to get too close, you know. I thought I might hurt you or something. You look like you just came home from Desert Storm," he joked, and then his expression changed to one of alarm. "Please tell me he didn't have anything to do with this."

"Oh no Brian, David would never."

I needed to soothe my nerves. Just thinking about what I was about to convey to him caused tears to well up in my eyes again. Noticing this Brian moved closer and gently placed his arm around my shoulder, pulling me to him. I set my cup back on the coffee table, cuddled into him and began to tell him everything. I told him about Brooke's condition all that the doctors said. I also told him about David, how he has been there to help me out as much as I would allow since I didn't want to mislead him. Brian listened intently as I conveyed all the details about the past week. When I finished his only response was "Wow!"

I asked him what he was doing here and he told me he came back for me. After I left he felt there was nothing more for him there and he wanted to come back home and handle his business – meaning me. He told me how he had gotten a message just as Jeff dropped him off and he immediately headed over to my place. I hoped he didn't see me blush as I thought, yeah girl you hit the jackpot this time.

"So you think you are just going to show up on your white horse and…?"

"Look, I told you before I left and again when you came to see me that when I got home it was going to be me and you. I meant it," Brian said and reached for my chin. He gently lifted my face to his until our eyes met. "The ball is in your court. What's it gonna be?"

This was one of the few times in my life that I was speechless.

"I want this too, Brian," I said.

Brian pulled me to him and kissed me. As our lips parted, I searched his eyes for sincerity. When I saw what I was looking for I giggled and buried my head into his firm, broad chest. Brian laughed. I knew right then that this was it for good. Then I looked into Brian's eyes again, this time with a devilish grin.

"What?" Brian asked, responding to my grin.

"Nothing," I said as I thought about the fact that the moment he thought this damsel was in distress he raced over to check on me. "I missed you, that's all," I said.

"I missed you too."

Brian planted a few soft kisses over my face then turned me so that my back could rest on his chest. He gently lifted my fractured leg on to the couch. He caressed my shoulders with his strong hands, sliding the strap of my tank off of my shoulder with his fingers. With extra care, he led a trail of kisses down the side of my neck, stopping at my shoulder. His touch ignited a spark of heat within the center of me. Brian continued his trail of tender kisses along the length of my arm as he entwined his fingers with mine. His continued along the back of my hand as he proceeded to kiss each finger one by one. He handled my fractured pinky with special attention.

Brian seamlessly returned his attention to my neck and shoulders, stirring up more than just emotions. My back arched, affording greater access to the sensitive zone. A slight moan escaped my lips

Pulling me in closely, Brian wrapped his arms around me,

sending heated sensations throughout my being. Releasing the hold, he firmly caressed my breasts while his tongue danced upon my neck and shoulders. I arched my back again signaling my authorization of free reign. Brian continued to caress my breast with one hand as the other traced circles along my abdomen. My insides tensed in erotic anticipation. Brian had moved on to trace the outline of my center as my feminine juices began to moisten the walls of my womanhood. Brian's firm hand covered me fully as he rubbed life into my core. His fingers stirred along the inner side of my thighs. Brian continued stroking then slowed down inserting one of his fingers, strumming my most sensitive spot with his thumb. Pleasure-induced purrs permeated from my throat. Detecting the heightened yearning, Brian stoked and strummed until I was panting and glowing from perspiration. I moaned louder. I felt pressure build, forcing my eyes to open and my back to arch involuntarily.

"Oh my...I'm gonna..." I sputtered relishing in the sensation that was pervading through my body.

Brian covered my mouth with a deep passionate kiss, stifling my screams of passion. My body upper body shuddered while steady spasms erupted through me one after the other until I was completely spent. I lay in Brian's arms basking in the afterglow.

Brian   CHAPTER 26

I did not look forward to seeing Shelly. However I knew that I had
to take care of the situation as soon as possible. The whole thing
didn't add up to me. As far as I was concerned, Shelly was intent on
playing games with me. I couldn't understand why she was so
pressed to break me down. She was surprised when I called her to
suggest we meet. I asked her why she was so surprised to hear from
me since she left messages with almost everyone we knew mutually.
I was pretty pissed about her spreading my business the way she did.
I asked her to meet me at the Starbucks across the street from
Bryant Park. I didn't want to meet at a restaurant or at my house.
The last thing I needed was a setting that could influence or mislead her in any way.

The Starbucks we met at was too small to have a confidential
conversation. Bryant Park was usually filled with the local business
people, which is why I chose that location. I assumed, rather I
hoped, she would be civil in these surroundings.

I saw Shelly approaching as she sauntered across the Avenue
of the Americas from the west side of Forty-Second Street. My eyes
bulged at the site of her protruding belly. I wasn't prepared for
what she would look like in person. A wave of anxiety overcame me.
I thought of Lexie. I didn't want anything to get in the way and

RENEE FLAGLER

mess us up.

Shelly reached for the door then retreated to allow a petite woman to exit before she stepped in. She looked beautiful. Shelly's usually curly hair was parted in the center and flowed endlessly down either side of her face. Her make up was light, which complimented her fresh look. A pinkish gloss decorated her full lips. She wore a pink wrapped maternity dress which clung to her feminine lines as well as her plump belly.

No matter how beautiful she looked, I knew the madness that loomed behind the beauty so I wasn't fazed. I raised my hand to signal where I stood and Shelly gaily walked over to me. She awkwardly wrapped her arms around my neck causing me to slightly stumble. She was being the bubbly Shelly that I knew when we first started seeing one another. Her glow was very evident up close.

150

"Hi Brian, sweetie," she sang. I felt my stomach churn. From the sound of her voice I knew I was in for some shit. She acted as if nothing had transpired. I wondered if she ever received those couch pillows.

Unable to match her gaiety, I replied evenly, "Hello Shelly, you look great." She placed her left hand across her lips to suppress a giggle, displaying a huge rock on her slender ring finger. The ring looked like something out of the Flintstones.

"You think so? Thank you, sweetie," she sang as she spun around, with her wrists flapping in the wind as she modeled for me. Shelly threw her head back and released a hearty laugh.

"You're looking fab yourself there, buddy. What have you been up to?" she asked and stepped back to take me in from head to toe.

Shelly smiled as if she was approving how I looked. My outfit was simple in comparison. I didn't want to look as though I was trying to remind her of what she was missing. My deep blue denim suit, beige cable-knit sweater and wheat-colored work boots were strictly for comfort.

"How far are you?" I asked.

"I'm in my eighth month," she said proudly. I quickly counted back eight months to February and realized there may be a chance. I also knew that there were other contenders since we were never in a committed relationship and both of us were seeing other people.

So Shelly, you're saying that this is my baby?" I shot straight, hoping to set the tone. Maybe she would pick up on that and shoot straight with me. Instead she stammered, but quickly regrouped.

"Yes sir," she said. Her gaiety had returned. I was puzzled.

"Shelly are you sure? I mean, we haven't been together for months," I said.

"What are you trying to say, Brian? I can't keep track of who I have sex with?" Shelly scowled.

I looked around to see if anyone had heard what she said. I was intent on not backing down.

"I am not concerned with who you 'screw,' Shelly. My concern is whether or not that baby you're carrying is mine. We haven't been together for months and all of the sudden you resurface, pregnant, and it's supposed to be mine?"

Shelly's mouth dropped and she began shaking her head back and forth.

"Brian, how could you? If I said it's yours, then it's yours. I can't believe you are accusing me of lying. And what do you mean by you don't care who I screw?"

She dramatically placed one hand on her belly as if to protect the ears of her unborn child and placed the backside of her free hand on her forehead as she continued.

"You know, I thought you would be happy to hear about our baby. I tried and tried to get in touch with you to let you know, but you were nowhere to be found. That's the reason I started to leave messages with people, because I couldn't find you. And no one would tell me where you were." Then in an instant her tone changed as she pleaded, "Brian sweetie, this is our chance to start over you, me and our new baby. Don't you see?"

I stood up before she could finish, unable to speak myself. Thick saliva held my mouth clamped shut. Now I know what a dog feels like when it foams at the mouth. I couldn't believe my ears. Shelly continued but I had no clue what she said. I took a deep breath in a useless attempt to collect myself before speaking.

"Shelly, where is this coming from? It has been over for a long time. Here you are talking about starting over. You prance up in here with a fucking rock as big as the North Star. Where is your man?"

Shelly grabbed for my hand in desperation as tears began to filter from her eyes. She didn't bother to wipe them away.

"Brian, don't worry about him. There is no 'him,' I put this on to make you jealous. I wanted you to think that there would be a chance of you losing me...of losing us." She gestured towards her belly. "Brian, we can work this out. I promise. I tried to get to you before now. For months, I tried to reach you. I called your work numbers, home and cell phone. I even stopped by your mother's house."

My anger mounted when she said that.

"Then when I couldn't find you anywhere, I got in touch with Jeff and told a few people to let you know I was looking for you. Don't you see Brian this is our second chance?" she whined.

"Who said I wanted a second chance with you?" I yelled.

I had both hands holding up my head. I thought it would burst. This scene was beginning to escalate and I had to bring it back down. Shelly began screaming and crying. She stood and began to wave her hands wildly as she continued to rant and rave, like a spoiled seven-year old child. I laced my fingers together under my chin and thought about my next move. Shelly continued her antics. I knew that couldn't be good for the baby. We had begun to gain the attention of bystanders. I had to bring the situation under control. I grabbed Shelly by her arms and told her to calm down and that we could talk about this. I didn't want to do this but I told her we needed to go somewhere private to talk so she could calm down. She needed to stop working herself up for the sake of the baby.

Shelly began to settle as I held her and tried to think of a private place. I was not about to take her to my house. I thought about an area hotel and quickly dismissed that idea. I hailed a taxi and gave him the address to Shelly's place.

When we got inside of Shelly's apartment, she started up all over again and began hyperventilating. I got scared and didn't know what to do. I ran to her kitchen for a paper bag but could only find plastic bags. I said what the hell. I would just make sure she doesn't suffocate. After getting Shelly to calm down again, I poured her a glass of water. I knew that I wouldn't be able to accomplish anything now.

Shelly sat slouched on the couch with tasseled hair and a wide-eyed look. I knew that she would be okay.

"Look Shelly, I didn't want to upset you. I just want to be sure. If the baby is mine, I have no qualms about caring for it."

Shelly stared aimlessly around the room and rolled her eyes without responding.

"All I want is a blood test. I have no intention of eluding my responsibilities as a father." I paused trying to think of what to say next. Nothing came to mind. "If you need anything, let me know."

I left feeling like I just spent a hard ninety seconds in the ring with Mike Tyson.

Lexie   CHAPTER 27

After a series of anxious knocks, Brian came barging into my house looking flustered. I intended to spend the afternoon with Brooke at the hospital but didn't want to say that to Brian. I didn't want him to think I was putting him off.

Brian walked past me, dropped himself down on the couch and buried his head in his hands. I sat beside him and gently rubbed his back.

"Whatever is, it will be all right, partner," I assured him, trying to offer some encouragement.

He remained silent then turned with a start and abruptly embraced me. I held him back. He released the hold and grabbed me by each arm.

"Babe, I need to know, are you with me no matter what?"

I guess I didn't answer fast enough because he repeated himself with much vehemence.

"Yes baby. I'm with you. You're my partner, remember?" I smiled, attempting to calm him.

"No matter what? I need you right now. I need to know that you are with me, no matter what happens," he said, holding my arms tighter.

"I'm here, babe. I've got you partner."

Brian managed a meek smile before a quick, snug embrace. He kissed me and left. I sat there wondering, what the hell was that about? I struggled to raise my derriere off the couch in search of my crutches. It was time to go see Brooke. I spent most of the late morning in the kitchen cooking up shrimp creole, one of Brooke's favorite dishes.

When I arrived on Brooke's floor I could hear her laughter flowing through the corridor. I smiled at the nurses at the station and kept moving towards Brooke's room.

"Damn, girl, I hear you all the way down the hall. You've got a party going on in here?" I teased.

Brooke smiled and held a finger up to me signaling she would be right with me. She had been on the phone and was wearing a hands-free ear-piece. I just shook my head. I wouldn't be surprised if Brooke's ear fell off due to extensive phone usage. I never knew anyone who loved the phone as much as she did.

Brooke's room looked like a flower shop, brimming with cheerful arrangements, balloons and get well wishes. I had our lunch set up by the time she ended her call.

"Who were you speaking to that had you giggling all over the place? I know it had to be someone of the male persuasion," I said.

"Don't hate the player, girl. Hate the game!"

"Yeah, 'playa' my ass. I would like to see a few of them roll up here to see you all at the same time," I joked.

Brooke burst out laughing.

"Now wouldn't that be something," Brooke said and continued laughing. "Girl you can't tell me anything. Here I am all broken up in a hospital bed and still have the guys trying to woo me from afar. Ooh, how hot am I?" I laughed, but little did she know the "broken up" comment stung.

I spent the rest of the afternoon with Brooke eating, joking, doing her nails and talking boy-talk. I updated Brooke on the situation with Brian and David. Brooke updated me on her condition and shared with me how much she looked forward to going to therapy. I assumed it was due to her recovery but managed to unveil the real reason. Earlier that day she had received a visit from her new physical therapist. Brooke advised that he was fine as hell and quite possibly unattached. I could picture Brooke flirting with him as he tried to tend to her medical needs.

I left Brooke well after visiting hours. We were fast asleep when the nurses came in to take her pressure and temperature for the umpteenth time. The nurses knew me well and never pressured me for staying after visiting hours were over. Knowing I was involved in the accident as well, the staff was sympathetic, and I imagine they also sensed my guilt.

When I reached home, the message indicator flashed like lights from a fire truck, signaling a full message box. I couldn't imagine why I had so many messages, until I realized I had left my cell phone on the coffee table. My cell phone message indicator flickered just as brightly as my answering machine. I checked the messages on my cell phone first. There were two messages from David, and one each from Ava and my mom. I decided to check my home line before calling anyone back. There were several hang ups, David requesting we get together to talk, my mother again and two unfamiliar voices. There was still no message from Brian, who I hadn't heard from since he barged in on me earlier.

One of the messages left by an unfamiliar voice, sounded as if the person could have been crying. The second message literally, knocked me off my feet.

"Hello Lexie, this is Shelly, Brian's baby's mother...well soon to be baby's mother. I am calling your number because I was trying to reach Brian. I assumed he would have come by your place to let you in on the great news. Anyway, I am on my way to the hospital. Our little bundle of joy may have decided to arrive a little early. If he does happen to come by do have him call me ASAP. Ciao. Oh and..."

The machine cut her off.

I was dumbfounded. I tried to move my legs to make my way over to the couch and couldn't. Tears began to flow like torrents and my heart felt as though it would soon burst right through my chest. Anger and pain fought to take precedence among my emotions. I made the attempt to narrow the distance between myself and a solid structure such as the couch. My broken leg proved to be more dependable than the other. As soon as I made my first step I stumbled and collapsed onto the floor nearly hitting my head on my coffee table. This enraged me even more.

Now I knew what was wrong with Brian when he came barging into my place. I had to figure this whole thing out. From what I knew about Shelly, this could all be a game but I refused to play the fool. Questions raced through my head as I tried to put things together. Was she really pregnant? If so, exactly how far? Was this Brian's baby? Was I being played? How did this bitch get my number? Why didn't he tell me about this? Where the hell was Brian? Why would she call my house looking for him?

Then I started answering my own questions —aloud.

"She's pregnant with that lying-ass Brian's baby. I can't believe he didn't tell me."

I knew things were going too well I just hadn't expected any-thing so soon. I needed to talk to Brian, someone, anyone. I want-ed answers.

I tried Brian's cell number only to get voicemail. I immedi-ately redialed the number several more times. The greeting began to get on my nerves. I tried to keep my cool. After a few more min-utes my house phone rang and the display identified Brian's cell number.

I snatched the phone off of the base.

"You need to tell me what the hell is going on." I yelled.

I was shocked when I heard Shelly's voice.

"Oh, is this Alexia? I thought I recognized the number. I am sorry but Brian is not available right now."

The next thing I knew the line was dead. I felt the steam rise within me.

Girlfriend thought she was being real cute, but I had news for her and Mr. 'Are-You-With-Me.' This was obviously the reason Brian hadn't called all day. He must have been with his new baby's mama.

Although I was pretty sure that I loved Brian, I was ready to cut my losses and get the hell out of Dodge.

I marched around the apartment gathering anything that belonged to Brian so that when he finally arrived to tell me the "great" news, I could hand him his things and show his ass the door. The thought of not being with him spurred a fresh batch of tears. I wiped them hard and fast. I wouldn't allow myself to be broken. I placed everything that belonged to Brian in a plastic bag and set it by the door. I returned to the couch to contemplate my next move. I still hadn't heard from Brian and I had reached a point far beyond anger.

I decided to call one last time and leave him a nasty message. After that he would never have to call me again. He could then go on to live his life happily ever after with his new baby's mama. Luckily the wicked-bitch-of-the-east didn't answer and I commenced to lace his voicemail with venomous expressions of pure contempt. The line had to be on fire by the time I was done. I didn't have the energy to make it to my bedroom and simply grabbed the nearest couch pillow and my beige chenille throw to cover myself. I cuddled up on the couch and stared into darkness until I was sound asleep.

The ringing telephone invaded my dreams. I woke with a start and quickly surveyed the room to verify the time. The DVD flashed twelve o'clock, but I was certain that it was way past that hour. I snatched the cordless phone and depressed the talk button forcibly. Unfortunately I couldn't demonstrate my irritation as well as I could with a corded telephone. Pressing the talk button really hard didn't quite send the same message as snatching a phone off the hook or slamming it into the cradle. I had to send the message of my exasperation by the tone of my greeting.

"Do you know what time it is?" I spat into the receiver.

I was famous for saying this as opposed to hello when someone took the liberty of calling my house at an ungodly hour. I could sense the caller's dithering. I hadn't bothered to look at the call ID display since it really didn't matter who was calling. Everyone was subject to the same objectionable greeting at this hour.

"Lexie," Brian simply stated.

The sound of his voice made me angrier. I opened my mouth to speak and tears sprang from my eyes. I closed my mouth determined not to reveal my raw emotions.

"Baby, what's up? Why did you leave me that message?"

I couldn't believe my ears. He had to be out of his mind. I was about to hit him with some serious 'sailor-speak' when I took notice of his distant tone.

"First of all, I had to have called you at least fifteen times, left you numerous messages and here you are just getting back to me during the wee hours of the morning. I guess you didn't have time for me since you were handling things with your new little family. But that's okay, Brian. I see that you have other plans on your agenda. You can come and get your shit out of my place anytime. I have already packed it all up for you!"

"Can I come by?" Brian asked.

He appeared to be unmoved by my little speech.

I couldn't help thinking that he must not have heard what I said. I positioned the phone like a walkie-talkie so that I could speak directly into it and yelled, "HELLO, IS THIS THING WORKING? ARE WE ON THE AIR? Did you miss everything I just said?"

I began to pant like a dog in heat.

"Lexie, can I come by? I need to talk to you," Brian said, remaining calm, only this time he was a little more insistent.

I couldn't believe this bird. I was furious.

"I guess you didn't hear me..."

"I heard you," Brian stated coolly.

"Whatever."

"Thank you. Now can you get up to open the door?"

As I sprung up from the couch, a pain shot straight through my injured leg. I eased back down took a deep breath and tried again, this time with more caution. I quickly hopped into the bathroom to brush my teeth, wash my face and check out how I looked. My ponytail hung to the center of my shoulder blades. The sides were a little tousled but ultimately, I liked the way it looked. The tank top and gray sweatpants I wore would have to do. I threw on my fluffy yellow slippers and hopped back into the living room. Just as I reached for one of my crutches there was a knock at the door. With the support of a single crutch I made it to the door opened it, and turned away without speaking a word. I walked back to the couch, sat, and picked up the remote to turn on the television. Without uttering a single word, I set the channel on BET, returned the remote to the coffee table and began watching as if I were alone.

Brian stood over me, watching me closely. He picked up the remote, hit the mute button, and sighed as he sat next to me on the couch. Finally I looked into his direction and felt a lump in my throat. I refocused my attention to the now silent TV.

"Your things are in that black bag by the door."

Brian dropped his head and took a deep long breath.

"I guess I know what your nasty little message was all about."

I turned towards him with an expression of mock surprise.

"Oh do you?" I inquired.

"Yes I do." Brian raised his eyes and smirked.

The expression on my face had to speak volumes about what I felt of his audacity. Brian looked at me and released a quick frustrated laugh. I rolled my eyes because I couldn't imagine anything being funny.

"Look Lexie, after I received your message I knew I needed to talk to you right away. I wanted you to have the full story before this whole thing got out of hand."

My focus and glare stayed with the silent images passing along the television before me.

"Yes, Shelly is pregnant," he admitted.

Those words caused my heart to leap and my lungs filled with air. Stubborn tears assembled in the wells of my eyes, determined not to fall. I tried to concentrate on the blurred images on the TV. I wanted to zone him out completely and at the same time I was eager to hear more.

"Listen Lexie, she says that it's mine, but I am not totally convinced. And don't think for a minute I am trying to dodge responsibility here." He sighed. "It has been a long time since Shelly and I had been together and you know this. She's actually close to her due date and I have to admit, with her being this far along, there may be a possibility that I am the father."

163

I couldn't hold back the tears any longer yet my gaze didn't waver. The silent tears rolled down my cheeks decorating my tank top with transparent pear-shaped droplets. I wanted him to stop talking.

"I met with her earlier today to discuss the whole thing and that didn't go very well. She caused a scene and I...let's just say the discussion didn't go well at all. I told her that if the baby is in fact mine, I would take care of it, but I want proof. I also told her that there was no chance of us getting back together." Brian paused and took another deep breath. "Sometime today I lost my cell phone. My head wasn't right, and I didn't even notice it until Shelly called Jeff's house this evening saying that she was going to the hospital because she was having complications. I asked why she called Jeff and she said because she had tried to reach me on my cell and I wouldn't answer. Then I used Jeff's phone to check my messages and that's when I heard your message. I went to Shelly's house to get my phone then came straight here."

"I want to be with you, Lexie. That's why I came here earlier to make sure that you would be willing to stick with me through thick and thin. But I see now that you are not as thorough as you say you are. At the first sign of trouble you want to throw my things in a bag without even hearing what I had to say."

I got up and pressed the message button on my answering machine to let Brian hear the message Shelly left. He sat in awe as the message played. His eyes narrowed from fury. Once the message ended, Brian immediately headed for the door.

"Brian, I don't know how to deal with all of this," I said and shrugged by shoulders.

Brian, quickly stepped back towards me, lifted my chin, moistened his lips and planted a sweet peck on mine.

"We will find a way," he said and headed out the door.

I just rolled my eyes.

Brian   CHAPTER 2 8

Shelly called to ask if I would accompany her to a prenatal visit. I was still upset about the stunt she pulled with Lexie and my cell phone, so I cordially declined. She immediately went into one of her frequent, oversensitive fits and started whimpering. She claimed she didn't have anyone to go with her.

"Who's been going with you?" I asked

"Never mind that, no one else is available. I need you to come with me." She wasn't budging. "Brian, please, I won't ask again, I promise. Besides this can be an opportunity for you to ask the doctor questions about the paternity tests," she said. That did it. I was going.

Shelly gave me the location of the doctor's office, and I told her I would meet her there. I had scheduled a meeting with a client for whom I was going to build a website. I needed to call to reschedule the appointment for a later time. Fortunately business had begun to pick up for me since I returned home. I called a few people to let them know that I was back in business developing IT applications, web sites and providing system maintenance services. I managed to drum up a nice piece of business for myself and began the process of incorporating my new company, B-IT Solutions.

Shelly's doctor was located in downtown Brooklyn in the Williamsburg area. The office was eclectically decorated with an afro centric flair. Beautiful art and exotic artifacts lined the walls in the waiting area. Despite the exquisite décor, the office had a warm and welcoming feeling to it. Shelly informed me that her doctor, a well-known medical professional, knew her parents well. She had been featured in the a few local and national publications and was named one of the top black doctors in the tri-state area.

From the array of faces in her waiting room, I could tell this doctor has crossed racial barriers. I felt a deep sense of pride and immediately developed great respect for this woman. I looked forward to meeting her.

Finally it was Shelly's turn to go in. I turned towards her to make sure she heard them call her name since she was chatting away on her cell phone. She motioned for me to accompany her and I violently shook my head no. Without stopping her conversation, Shelly grabbed my hand to pull me up. Despite my obvious resistance, Shelly tugged harder. Realizing that I had no intention of budging, Shelly asked the party on the other line to hold for a moment

"Don't you have questions for the doctor?" she asked.

I reluctantly got up and accompanied Shelly through the door separating the waiting area from the examination rooms. Shelly took this opportunity to grab hold of my hand. I started to pull away from her and thought about my gesture either embarrassing her or setting off her drama meter. I decided to let her have her moment and figured it couldn't cause any damage within the confines of the doctor's office. I immediately regretted my decision when I saw Lexie's sister, Dionne, exiting one of the examination rooms. I slyly dropped Shelly's hand, hoping that Dionne didn't notice. I closed my eyes wishing I was anywhere else but here.

I decided it would probably be in my best interest to speak.

"Hey D, what's up?" I greeted her with a friendly peck on the cheek.

"Not much Brian, how are you?" she said before taking another look in Shelly's direction.

Shelly was now staring both of us up and down. Dionne cut her eyes at Shelly.

"Well Brian, I need to be on my way. Will you see Lexie, later?"

"Yes," I said coolly.

"Great. Could you have her call me please? Thanks, and take care of yourself," she said before swiftly departing.

I knew I would hear about it later.

"Who was that?" Shelly asked with an attitude.

I smiled and ignored her. She huffed and stormed into the designated examination room. I could feel her shooting daggers at me with her eyes. I continued to ignore her. It was none of her business and for some reason the scene became a bit comical to me, but laughing at that very moment would be sure to ignite her. I kept my cool, while Shelly prepared for the doctor's arrival. When Dr. Martin entered the room, Shelly was sitting at the edge of the examination table undressed from the waist down. Her arms were crossed at her chest and she sported a childish pout. I greeted Dr. Martin and introduced myself.

Dr. Martin proceeded with an internal examination and sonogram. I was amazed at the images of the baby moving along the black and white screen. I became further engrossed when the doctor placed some sort of monitor on Shelly's belly that allowed us to hear the baby's heart beat. Something I couldn't explain came over me. For the first time since hearing about Shelly's pregnancy, it didn't seem so bad that the baby could be mine. I found out that Shelly was a few weeks away from delivering. Once the exam was complete the doctor told Shelly that everything looked great and asked if she had any questions. Shelly said, "No." Dr. Martin then advised Shelly that she could get dressed and turned to exit the room.

I thought about what I needed to ask just as Dr. Martin reached the door.

"Excuse me Dr. Martin," I said.

Shelly shot me a look of contempt. I paid her no mind.

"I have a few questions I would like to ask, doctor," I continued.

"Sure, how can I help you?" Dr. Martin replied.

Shelly began putting her clothes back on with haste. Just as I thought that it would best to speak with the doctor in private.

"Brian, don't you think that can wait?" Shelly asked. I smiled trying to control myself in front of the doctor.

"No Shelly, I don't think it can. That's why I am here today isn't it?" Then I turned to the doctor and asked, "Could I talk to you for a moment in private?"

"We can talk in my office. It's right at the end of hall. Can you give me a few minutes? I'll meet you there," she said.

"Sure," I said and smiled.

I could feel the heat of Shelly's eyes on the back of my neck.

As soon as Dr. Martin closed the door behind her, Shelly launched towards me, beating my chest with her fists. I tried to grab hold of her hands amidst her wild swinging.

"Why are you doing this Brian, I told you it's your baby."

I was rapidly reaching the end of my rope with her. I grabbed her by both arms and shook her. Shelly's ranting turned to wailing.

"Shelly, what the hell is wrong with you? Didn't you tell me to come so that I can talk to the doctor? Now you wanna flip out? I'm sick of you and your games."

I was out of control and Shelly just stared at me with fear in her eyes.

"I can't do this anymore," I yelled and let her go.

I started pacing around the tiny room. Shelly backed up against the wall. I was sure that people were probably gathered outside the door listening, but this time I didn't care. I took a deep breath and commenced to letting her have it.

"I am going to talk to that doctor, find out what I need to know and I'm out. Don't call me and ask me to come to the doctor anymore. I don't want to hear shit from you until I know if I am the father or not. And so help me, after all that you have been putting me through you'd better hope I'm the father!"

I swung open the door and charged towards Dr. Martin's office, leaving Shelly standing with her mouth open. It felt good to finally stand up to her instead of giving in to her antics. Keeping the peace was keeping me stressed.

I could sense the curiosity in Dr. Martin's eyes before asking my first question. I explained the nature of my request. Dr. Martin didn't appear to be surprised. She proceeded to explain to me that a DNA paternity test can be performed immediately after the baby is born. She further explained that there were two types of tests, one that used cheek cells and a blood test. Both tests provided very accurate results indicating the probability of paternity greater than ninety-nine percent. The results can be determined within ten days. She advised me of the steps I needed to take and the cost. I thanked

169

her and headed for the door. By the time I came out of the office, Shelly was gone. I proceeded to my appointment.

When I got home, Shelly was sitting in her car in front of my apartment. I shook my head and wondered if the drama would ever cease. Shelly got out her car and trotted over to me. Her demeanor was sweet, as if the events of earlier were merely a delusion. I know I scared her before so I was careful now. As she approached me, she dropped her head.

"Hi Brian, I was wondering if we could talk."

I had a little time before going over to Lexie's, so I agreed. I decided then to stay with Lexie tonight if she would have me. I didn't want Shelly coming back.

When we reached my apartment, I invited her in and asked if she wanted anything to drink. She declined my offer and sat on the couch fiddling her thumbs. I wanted her to get a move on so I asked what she wanted to talk about.

"Brian, I apologize for my behavior in the Dr. Martin's office. I also apologize for my erratic behavior in general and thank you for coming today. It's just that I want things to work out for us the best way it can. I am confident that once the baby is here, you will see things my way. It's just that I get so upset when you bring up the possibility that the baby is not yours."

"Well Shelly, the possibility exists, doesn't it?" She sighed and looked away. "Answer me Shelly!"

Shelly's shoulders slumped and tears began to fall from her eyes. I started thinking that the emotional roller coaster she had been on could not possibly be good for the baby.

"Brian I want this baby to be yours. I'm almost positive that it's yours." Shelly began rubbing her belly and smiled. "Come here."

She reached her hand out to me.

I was hesitant. She smiled again.

"Come on, I won't bite you."

I walked over to the couch and stood over her. She patted the seat cushion next to her, gesturing for me to sit down. I remained standing. She took my hand and placed it on her belly. I felt the baby move against my palm. My eyes closed involuntarily. Determined not to show her how it affected me, I excused myself. I went to my room to get a bag to throw a few things in for my stay at Lexie's place. I wished that it was Lexie's stomach that I laid my hand upon to feel the movement of our baby.

Shelly's presence was now making me uncomfortable. I was experiencing a change of heart pertaining to the baby and didn't know how to deal with it. I filled her in on my conversation with Dr. Martin. She said nothing in response. I asked Shelly if there was anything else she wished to discuss and told her that I needed to get going. She asked me where was I going and then answered her own question.

171

"You're probably going to Lexie's, right?" she asked.

This time I didn't respond. She asked if she could use the bathroom before she left. It took her a while but I assumed it was due to her pregnancy.

When I reached Lexie's house I looked for bags at the door. I told her about seeing Dionne today at the doctor's office and conveyed Dionne's message.

"Yeah, I heard," was her clipped response.

There was nothing for me to say. I decided to follow her lead. If she mentioned anything more about it then I would respond. I needed peace and that's usually what I had when I was with Lexie. But with all of the events of the past week things were a little more tense that usual. I needed to give Lexie a little time to absorb everything.

I wanted her to know exactly where she stood in my life. If I had a ring I would have proposed, even with her having an obvious attitude. I had to get to the bottom of this paternity thing soon. The tension in the room was so thick that you could cut it with a knife. Lexie readied herself for bed as if I wasn't even there. I figured it was best for me to sleep at my own place, so I left and went back home.

Lexie

CHAPTER 29

My old boss called and told me she had a job for me whenever I was ready. Her reputation placed her in demand amongst the competition. Once they became aware of her availability, one of our competitors contacted her to make an offer. She also received calls from several partnering companies. Finally she accepted a job as Vice President of Marketing and Sales at a well-known wireless competitor. In her position she would be responsible for all aspects of sales, marketing, advertising, promotions and events. She made me an offer I couldn't refuse. I would come on board under her as the new Assistant VP and Director of Marketing. I told her I would see her in two weeks with or without crutches.

I called Dionne to tell her the good news. Dionne decided to take the afternoon off so that we could meet for lunch and shop in celebration of new beginnings. We decided to have lunch at Ida Mae's, located in the heart of the fashion district and then head over to Macy's Herald Square for a little shopping.

It was a typical cool day for October, so I opted for a casual capri suit and matching lightweight three-quarter jacket. I slid on a comfortable, low-heeled ivory boot on the available foot and of course my cast, covered the other. I styled my hair in a simple pony tail and put on a pair of amber-tinted sunglasses. Despite the unfashionable cast, I was pleased. I blew a kiss at the girl staring back at me in the mirror and headed for the door.

When I arrived at Ida Mae's, I could see Dionne seated in the elegant lounge area, sipping on a cocktail. As I approached Dionne, I blatantly glanced at my watch and raised a brow at the refreshing cocktail sitting on the small table before her.

"This is a girl's afternoon out. I'm entitled," she said and laughed.

We decided to remain in the elegantly decorated lounge area and ordered drinks and appetizers. It felt great to get out. Not only was the décor incredible, the food was absolutely superb. I decided I would surprise Brian by bringing him there for dinner one evening, if things ever really worked out.

As we sat and chatted, Dionne asked how things were going with Brian. I sighed as I took a sip and placed my second glass of Pinot Grigio on the small table.

"Well Sis, despite the pregnancy twist, I guess things are okay. He's been putting in overtime to make me comfortable.

"So what's the problem?"

"I don't know how to deal with the whole thing with Shelly." I felt my mouth get dry. "I give new meaning to the cliché 'you have to take the good with the bad.' Look at David and I. Things were going very well. I thought he was the one and look at how he ended up hurting me. I never thought that would end the way it did."

Dionne put both hands in the air. "Wait, don't tell me that you are still aching over the whole situation with David? And further-more, please don't tell me that you are comparing the two of them."

"No," I blurted. "Trust me, I'm over David. But Brian seems too good to be true at times. Then everything took a turn. There is so much tension between us now. I really care about him but this baby has certainly but a damper on things just when things really started to heat up. I do admit he has been trying pretty hard."

"Wait. So what's the problem here?" Dionne questioned.

"Me, I guess." Dionne looked confused. "Whenever things are going very well in my life something happens to bring it all crashing down on me. It never fails. I've gotten to point in my life that when something good happens, I just sit back and wait for something horrible to happen next. Just look at my track record: David, my job and now Brian...even Brooke."

I felt like I was whining. I sipped the icy water the waiter brought to the table.

"You need to stop blaming yourself for Brooke's condition," Dionne scolded while pointing her finger at me.

Tears began to fall. Dionne took my hand in hers and reflected a moment.

"You know how people say you can speak things into existence?" She paused for me to respond but I didn't so she continued. "If you keep expecting things to go wrong, they will."

"You know what's worse?" I asked, wiping the tears away.

"What?"

"I think I love him, D," I finally admitted.

"Hey, what's so bad about that? You told me yourself you could see being with me forever. If you love him then you'll have to take the chance and ride this out." Dionne handed me a tissue from her bag and continued. "At least he is being a man about the situation with Shelly. If you were in her situation wouldn't you want the same? I know brothers who wouldn't give a second thought to walking away from this whole thing without looking back. He's determined to find out if the child is his so that he can do right by it."

"Maybe you're right." The truth is I am so tired of waiting for the worst. Even when you told me you saw them at the doctor's office, I expected things to fall apart. Not to mention I thought you would think I was a fool for still hanging around."

"Lexie, I'm not one to judge. Everyone has issues. You said he has outdone himself in trying to prove to you that you are what really matters to him. See what happens. You gotta take the good with the bad. Enjoy the good, and deal with the bad as it comes."

"You're right. But you don't think I am crazy for sticking with it?"

"That's for you to decide. I've got your back either way," Dionne said then paused as if an idea had just come to her. "Here we are on a girl's afternoon out, sulking!" We both laughed. "Correct me if I am wrong, but we did come out to celebrate something good, right? We should have our behinds in Macy's checking out some shoes. Girl let's go!"

Dionne motioned for the waiter and paid the tab. We hadn't even ordered our lunch.

When I got back home, I called Brian to invite him over for a nightcap. I wanted to get our relationship out of the lull that we have been in and move on. He said he would be there as soon as he finished a business dinner with his client.

I knew he had eaten, so I prepared something light. I set the table with candles, stemware and a chilled bottle of Kendal Jackson Chardonnay. On my way in, I picked up two pounds of prawns for shrimp cocktails. I seasoned the prawns lightly and steamed them just right. Then I made my fabulous homemade cocktail sauce.

By the time Brian rang my bell, I was ready for him. I was scandalously clad in a long black lounging gown with endless splits, revealing my cast and one sexy mocha brown leg. The gown provocatively caressed the curves of my body. I pulled my hair up into a bun so that it wouldn't get in the way and added a light glow of lip gloss.

Brian walked in with the most beautiful spray of lilies I had ever seen. He smiled and looked around the room nodding his approval.

"Hi," he said cautiously.

"Hi."

He kissed me softly, leaving a hint of moisture on my lips. The gentleness took my breath away.

Brian remained in his spot like a stranger waiting to be offered a seat. I took the flowers, closed my eyes and relished in the aroma emitting from them.

"I stopped at Blockbuster and picked up some movies," Brian said awkwardly.

"Okay."

I went into the kitchen to retrieve a vase and set the flowers on the dining table. Before making himself comfortable, Brian walked around to inspect the scene I created, smiling his approval.

"What did you get?" I asked,

"Some oldies but goodies. And don't laugh when I tell you which ones. I was just in the mood for some of the old stuff. I figured it would be fun."

"I won't laugh. Tell me what you've got."

Brian raised an eyebrow before responding, "I've got "Foxy Brown" with Pam Grier and "Disco Godfather" with Rudy Ray

Moore."

I fell out laughing and Brian pretended to be hurt.

"You said you wouldn't laugh."

"You have got to be kidding me. You want me to sit here with you and watch Dolemite and Foxy Brown?" I asked. Brian had to laugh.

"Yes. What's so wrong with that?"

"Fine with me," I said and tried my best to stop snickering.

Brian playfully nudged me and got up to bring the shrimp, cocktail sauce, wine and glasses over to the table so we could eat while we watched TV. First we watched the second-rate, yet extremely hilarious Dolemite movie in its entirety. By the end we were both bent over laughing and practically in tears.

Halfway through Foxy Brown, sparks of passion began to hover over us. The tension was gone. Brian leaned over careful of my healing leg and kissed me. Brian caressed my cheeks with the backside of his hand then proceeded to lightly run his fingers down the length of my torso, occasionally stopping to trace the outlines of my breasts, navel and hips. Brian then ran his hands along the splits in the side of my gown until he reached my hips. He pulled me closer to him and reached in to kiss me again. I eased up and took him by the hand to lead him to the bedroom. Brian swept me off my feet and carried me to the bed. He placed me down gently and undressed me. He planted sweet kisses all over me from head to toe before sliding me further on the bed and burying his face between my legs, quickly causing my body to shudder in ecstasy.

I undressed him and returned the favor until he arrived at the brink of his sensual crest. He lifted me up pulling himself from me. We joined bodies. Brian began to swear softly as he held me by my hips guiding our rhythm. I moaned loudly and gasped for air. The feel of Brian's body against mine drove me crazy. His steady, sensual rhythm developed into a quickened pace. I grabbed a pillow and filled my mouth to stifle the sound of pleasure-filled screams as I rapidly reached a point of eruption. Brian moved faster and deeper until we reached our sexual pinnacles together.

As my body convulsed from the sensation, nerves sent vibrations to the surface of my skin. His slightest touch ignited new sparks. I quaked from the currents racing through me. I could no longer bare the touch of his hands or the brush of his body against mine.

I tried to pull away trying not to be overtaken. He held on tighter and loved me even more fervently –refusing to let go. My voice was caught in violent gasps for air and tears seeped from my eyes. I was suspended in ecstasy. Brian still held on, now bucking wildly from his own delicious orgasm. His muscles tensed from spasms. The sensual hold released me and I floated back into my natural self. Never could I recall being loved to tears.

"I love you," I whispered.

I realized what I had just said only after the words betrayed my mind and escaped my lips.

Brian   CHAPTER 30

It was game day. The New York Jets were playing against the Miami Dolphins. A few of us guys were going over Jeff's place to watch the game on his new sixty-five inch, big-screen TV. I headed over a little early, determined to get a hold of Jeff's ear before the rest of our boys arrived. As I arrived, a cute stout chick was leaving his place. I offered a quick greeting and proceeded to the kitchen to put down the beer I brought. I could overhear Jeff and Ms. Stoutness exchanging goodbyes. Jeff promised he'd call after the game.

Jeff joined me in the kitchen wearing a sly smile.

"What," I asked.

He was waiting for me to ask about this one because I had never seen her before. In fact, like his shoes, I don't think I ever saw him with the same one twice. Jeff rubbed his goatee in anticipation.

"Go ahead and ask."

"I have nothing to say or ask," I said and laughed, while stocking the fridge with beer.

"You sure?"

I just stared at Jeff. I knew where this was going. For one thing, this woman was a little thick for Jeff's taste. Most importantly, Jeff does not usually have women at his place, and her presence didn't go unnoticed. Still I said nothing which made Jeff all the more curious. I was more concerned with why I had come over extra early to talk to him.

"All right man, if you say you have nothing to say, I'm cool with that," Jeff said.

"Okay man, what's up with the chunky chick?"

I tried hopelessly to stifle the laughter rising from my gut.

"See, I knew it. I knew you were going to have something to say. Man you don't know, that chick can burn. Check out what's in the pots." Jeff walked over to the stove. "She knew I was having my boys over for the game and she cooked up some buffalo wings, BBQ ribs and made potato salad. No pizza this time my man. We got real food."

"Damn," I said.

"All thanks to my shorty. I'm gonna be honest with you, man, I'm feeling her."

With a right hand in the air, I stopped Jeff in his tracks. "Man, you don't have to explain nothing to me," I assured him.

Eyeing me suspiciously, Jeff wasn't quite convinced since he was so used to me ragging on him about his choice of women. Unlike most of the others, this one was actually pretty cute. She was definitely plump in all the right places.

After filling the fridge with more beer, Jeff and I made our way back to his small living room. Jeff's place was a typical bachelor's pad with stark white walls, no curtains, and void of even the slightest hint of a woman's touch. Masculinity prevailed as evidenced by macho necessities such as calendars of women in bathing suits and a banging stereo system loud enough to uproot the dead.

We relaxed on the couch watching rap videos on MTV, purely for the girls more than the love of the music. After minutes of pondering where to start, I started with what had been foremost in my mind.

"Lexie told me she loved me," I said and Jeff raised his body from his slouched position on the couch.

"Whoa," was all he managed, so I continued knowing I had his full attention.

"Yeah man. That bugged me out. I don't know if she knows whether or not I heard her say it."

"So you didn't say anything in response?"

"No. Do you think that is good or bad?"

"Depends."

"On what?"

"If you love her back."

Jeff's statement just hung in the air for a while as I kicked the thought around in my head. I knew she was the one, but was I in love yet?

"Well do you?" Jeff asked.

"I think I do, but things are so complicated right now. I don't want her to get caught up in this bullshit with Shelly."

"If you want to be with Lexie and you are feeling her like that, then it shouldn't matter what comes of the baby situation."

"True, but things are a little more complex than that." I said. "I'm feeling Lexie, but I also feel a sense of obligation towards Shelly because of the baby."

"I guess I can see where you are going with that but still, I say, if Lexie is the one you want then why let anything stand in the way of that, whether the kid is yours or not?"

"I feel you man, but there's more."

"Shit, that was easy. Throw it at me."

Jeff told me to wait and grabbed two more beers from the

fridge then got comfortable, ready for me to unload the additional drama.

"Shelly's been following me around."

"She's stalking you?"

"I've noticed her hiding out in her car outside of my apartment. One night she followed me. I was on my way to Lexie's house and I headed for my mother's house instead."

"Damn!"

"One night she popped up and wanted me to make love to her. I told her no and she lost it."

"She's bananas."

"I just want to keep her away from Lexie. I can't wait until the baby is born. I'll find out if it's mine and that's it. Right now, I just stay away from her ass. I found out her due date from the doctor."

"When is it?"

"November sixteenth, but the doctor told me that she could have it two weeks before or two weeks after. The sooner the better, if you ask me."

"That's right around the corner," Jeff said and then paused.

"Yo, I got a new name for her, kid," Jeff said snickering.

"What, man?"

"Shycho. Get it, Shelly and psycho?" Jeff fell over on the couch laughing at his own corny joke.

The doorbell rang and we tabled our discussion. The rest of the guys came in at once weighted down with cases of beer. With everything I had on my mind. I couldn't even get into the game.

Lexie   CHAPTER 3 1

I had an appointment to see the doctor and have my cast removed. I was elated at the thought of being able to take a nice long soak in the tub and pretty anxious to shave my leg. I could only imagine the woolly mass that hid behind the cast. The intense itching I had endured for the past six weeks made me want to rip the cast and the leg apart piece by piece. I was so tired of wearing the cast that I felt as though its removal should be deemed a day worthy of national recognition.

I went to visit Brooke at the rehabilitation facility after my appointment. Although she wasn't fully walking on her own, her progress has been nothing short of miraculous. She was due to come home on Halloween. The relentless pain she long endured on a daily basis had virtually diminished to occasional discomfort. A love affair had also secretly blossomed between her and her physical therapist, one that was destined to remain undisclosed until she was discharged from the facility.

Brian promised to take me to dinner to celebrate the big day and the start of my new job on Monday. I couldn't wait to be able to wear a cute pair of shoes or boots. I was determined to look like a doll for our evening festivities. As for my visit to the doctor, I chose a comfortable heather gray sweat suit with a tank top and sneakers. The two piece set would be perfect coverage in the cool crisp autumn air. I donned the old faithful ponytail and threw on a pair of sunglasses.

My house phone rang twice and stopped, signaling that Brian was waiting for me out front. I grabbed my purse, a single crutch and keys as I headed out. Brian approached just as I turned the key to lock the door.

"You didn't have to come up partner I could have made it down on my own," I told him.

When I turned to face Brian I was momentarily struck by his arresting presence. He looked totally edible in a midnight blue suit, light blue dress shirt and matching silk tie. He must have just stepped out of the barber's chair with his sharply trimmed hairline and goatee.

185

"Mmm, don't you look yummy?" I sang as he leaned in to kiss me with those full luscious lips.

Brian returned a sly smile and asked, "Want a taste?"

"Just a taste? No honey, I want to sop you up with a biscuit and lick the plate clean," I teased and began licking my fingers greedily as if I just devoured a plate of BBQ ribs.

Brian chuckled as he took my arm to assist me out of the building.

I shouted, "Crip has left the building!"

After my doctor's appointment, Brian dropped me off to visit Brooke. When I walked in she was reading the book 'Slim Down Sister.'

"Now why on earth are you of all people reading that?" I quizzed.

Brooke was never one to have a problem with her weight. If

she merely thought about loosing five pounds, it would be done by the end of the week.

"I'm almost done with this therapy stuff. I need to get my body back together. Besides I have new motivation for the cause now." Brooke giggled as she discreetly referenced her newest lover and physical therapist.

"Who? Dr. Feel-Good?" I teased.

She threw a pillow at me. She still hadn't noticed that my cast had been removed. I deliberately strutted from one side of her bed to the other until the realization hit her.

"Oh my God Lexie, your cast is off. How do you feel? I bet you are going to have that leg hiked up in the air tonight. Aren't you?" Brooke teased. "Shoot, don't try and act like you won't. I know you better than you know yourself, remember?" That was true.

"All right already, I am an undercover freak. But it ain't nobody's business what I do," I replied in my best Billy Holiday impression.

I updated Brooke on the latest with Shelly.

"She ain't nothin' but a ham," Brooke said.

"A ham? I was puzzled.

"Yes girl, a Hot Ass Mess! What did Brian put on that girl?"

"Girl, I won't lie, the brother is packing. And Lord knows he's an expert at operating the machinery," I said, thinking about Brian in the bedroom. "Oh, did I tell you about the time he screwed my ass to tears. By the time we were done. I slipped up and told that brother, 'I love you.' I wanted to suck my thumb and call my momma."

"No you didn't. Are you serious?"

"I am dead serious! I am surprised I didn't tell you about that one." My cheeks were heated from blushing.

"Well then, that explains it. That's why the girl can't seem to get over him. He's packing a platinum rod. And, about this 'I love you' stuff? What is the deal with that? Do you really love him?"

I smiled and sighed at the thought. I really did love Brian. "Yes I do."

"Oh wait a minute. I guess I would too if I had a brother carting me off to exotic places on a moment's notice.

"You are too much, Brooke."

"Really, I am very happy for you and I wish my 'bestest' friend in the whole world the absolute grandest in love and happiness. Maybe one day I will get there myself."

"That was so sweet. You know I love you, right?

"Yeah, yeah. Enough of the mushy stuff." We both cracked up laughing.

I left Brooke shortly after Dr. Feel-Good returned for their late afternoon therapy session. I kept making faces and winking at Brooke from behind his back. While she tried her best to maintain a solid front, she failed sorely. He stared at each of us suspiciously, but every time he looked my way I feigned a look of innocence. Finally Brooke couldn't hold in her laughter any longer and threw a pillow in my direction.

"Get out of here," she yelled.

Just as I reached the door to my apartment, the urge to urinate hit me like a ton of bricks. Then the telephone started ringing. I hurried inside to snatch the phone off the hook before the person could hang up while performing the pee-pee dance.

"Hello...Hello! Damn!" No one said anything.

I slammed the phone down and quickly ran off to relieve

myself. As soon as I hit the damn bathroom the phone began to ring again. This time the person would just have to call back. Then my cell phone rang. I quickly handled my business because I knew that could have been no one but Brian. I raced back to the living room to get my cell out of my purse and answered immediately. I didn't bother looking to see who it was when I answered.

When I said 'hello,' the person sucked their teeth and hung up. I knew it was Shelly.

I ran a nice hot bath while deciding what to wear for my night out on the town with my lover-boy. I decided on a sexy chocolate brown wrap dress I picked up from a boutique while we were in France, a pair of tan sling backs with satin ribbons that tied around my ankle. The fragrance I chose for the evening was Jessica McClintock, my absolute favorite. The phone rang again and I pouted. This time it was Brian saying that he would be over to pick me up in less than an hour. I had to make it snappy.

I opted for a quick soak before getting dolled up. By the time I finished oiling my body, Brian was ringing the bell. Maybe I should give him a key, I thought. Then I thought again. I loved him, but damn. I grabbed a silky robe and ran to quickly unlock the door. When Brian stepped in, my jaw hit the floor. Words could not describe how good this man looked.

"Well, you are just one tall drink of water."

Brian slowly spun to showcase his attire. His tan single-breasted suit was the perfect compliment to my brown dress and tan accessories. His shirt hung slightly unfastened, revealing the upper portion of his sexy broad chest. I had to run and get myself together quickly. I couldn't wait to see the picture we made together. All eyes were sure to be on us.

When we got outside, Brian escorted me to the passenger door of his brand new silver Cadillac Escalade EXT.

"Boy, whose car have you stolen?" I teased.

"Let's just say business is going well," Brian said and laughed.

He had to help me into the oversized vehicle. The car was the first of a string of surprises that evening. We dined at the Water Club, a floating restaurant on the east side of Manhattan with breathtaking views of the East River. Dim lighting coupled with the glistening of the fireplace fashioned a setting of pure splendor.

When Brian and I finished our dinner, he decided we should order a glass of champagne for a toast. Moments later the waiter arrived with two crystal glasses filled the bubbly liquid. Brian raised his glass.

"To your new job, to no more casts..." I snickered at the notion of celebrating my cast removal as Brian continued his toast. "To my latest contract, the launch of my new business and most importantly, to us."

It was time for me to make a toast of my own.

"To new beginnings, to great expectations..." and I echoed Brian's sentiments with "and most importantly, to us."

Brian beamed and we sipped from our glasses together. My glass appeared to have something in it. When I inspected it further I gasped. Inside there was a delicate necklace of white gold adorned by a diamond pendant in the shape of a pad lock.

"Oh my God, Brian, I can't believe you." I extracted the stunning piece and admired it through misted eyes. "You didn't have to do this...but I'm glad you did," I joked. "But really you didn't. This is absolutely beautiful."

"You're welcome. You know what this means right?" he asked

as he placed the necklace around my neck.

"Is this your way of saying you have me locked down, Mr.? I slapped his hand playfully before leaning in to give him a soft thankful kiss.

"Pretty much!" Brian teased. The next statement nearly knocked my socks off. "Don't think that I didn't hear you the other night."

I knew exactly what he was talking about and I was stunned. Ever since the "I love you" slip, neither of us has dared to mention it. I wondered why he brought it up now. As if he read my mind he continued.

"It's all good though, because I feel you on that one."

I knew brother man was not trying to say I love you with out actually saying it. Oh no, I will not be cheated.

"Baby, are you trying to say something to me?" I was going to pull it out of him if I had to.

"All right, you got me."

"Come on with it, partner. Don't cheat me."

"All right, All right!" Brian took my hand into his, looked directly into my eyes and said those three words that made my heart flutter. "Lexie, I love you."

"Oh Brian, I love you too." He couldn't have picked a more perfect setting.

Brian and I made it. It felt so wonderful to hear him say those words.

After that we went dancing. We ended our night of grandeur back in Brooklyn with breakfast at a local diner then watched the sun rise.

Brian   CHAPTER 32

After working out I took a shower and just threw on a pair of box-ers. It was Saturday and Lexie was spending the day with her mom and sisters. Jeff had taken Ms. Stoutness to Atlantic City for the weekend so I decided to stay home and chill. I planned to sit around all day watching movies and drinking beer.

When my phone rang I knew it had to be either my mom or Shelly. I hoped it was my mother. Shelly was at the point where she was likely to go into labor at any given moment. She called nonstop, trying to sway me into making a decision about her and the baby. Now that I had caller ID I could tell who was calling. The call reg-istered as S. Winston. Shelly. I thought about not answering but reconsidered because she was so close to her due date. I braced myself and picked up attempting to sound cheerful.

"Hey Shelly, what's up? Feeling all right?"

"Yes. I just wanted to hear your voice. What are you doing?" she asked and I sighed.

"I was just about to go check out my mother. She needed a few things from the store." I amazed myself at how quickly that lie rolled off of my tongue.

"Oh, how about I go with you?"

"Nah, that's okay. Listen I gotta run, all right," I said, hoping to run her off the phone, but Shelly went on as if I had said 'so tell me what's on your mind.'

"Brian, I have been thinking. I don't think you're taking me seriously. I really mean it when I say it's you, me and the baby or nothing at all. You won't even have to bother telling your little crippled girlfriend. I would take great pleasure in delivering that message."

The fact that she knew that Lexie had been in a cast alarmed me. I wondered if she had been spying on her as well. If so, it wasn't too recent since Lexie's cast had been removed. This girl was giving me migraines. I tried to tread lightly just long enough to get the paternity tests and get the results.

"Shelly, what's up? Is that what you called me for?"

"Not exactly." She changed her tone to one more sane and soft. "Brian sweetie, I am sorry, I don't mean to pressure you. I am certain you will make the right decision honey…" Shelly paused and I could hear her gasping.

I sat straight up and yelled into the phone "Shelly…Shelly." "Are you okay? Are you in labor?"

"Oh Brian, I need you. I think this is it," then she screamed.

"All right, Shelly, I am on my way. "

I quickly got dressed and headed over to Shelly's place. By the time I reached her door she was standing in the entrance wearing a sheer shirt, panties and a flowing silk robe. There was no doubling over, no look of pain nor a trace of discomfort. I was pissed. There I was, driving across town like a bat out of hell and she was playing games.

"What the hell is this about, Shelly?"

"I knew you cared sweetie, come on in."

"No, I am not coming in. Why did you do this?" I thought

about it and decided I didn't even want to know why. "You know what? Scratch that question, I don't care."

I turned to leave when Shelly ran after me and grabbed my arm.

"Brian, please don't leave." That's when the waterworks started.

"Listen, I don't have the time or the energy for you. Now let go of me," I said through clenched teeth.

"No, Brian. Please don't go. That's the only way I could get you over here."

"What?" I was baffled. "You did all of this just to get me over here?"

Shelly lowered her head as she nodded and loosened the grip she had on my arm.

"Please," she pleaded, "Just come in for a moment so we can talk."

"Just make it quick." I spat. When I agreed to come in her face lit up. I walked in and stood by the door. She offered me a seat and something to drink. I refused both.

"Are you just going to stand there?"

"Yeah, so you might as well start talking. I've got some business to take care of."

She was getting frustrated, but I couldn't care less. I was tired of being strung along while having to walk on egg shells as she toyed with me.

"Okay, Brian." She took a seat on her white leather sofa. "Whenever I ask you to come by you tell me you can't. If I come by your place or simply call you are always just on your way out. And you won't come to the doctor with me anymore. How else could I get to you? I am sorry for what I did, but you left me no alternative."

Shelly got up and started pacing before she continued.

"Brian, I really need to know what it is that you want to do. I want to have a family – a complete family. I want it to be you, me and our baby. It was so good with you in the past Brian, I just want that back."

I looked to the heavens for strength and decided to take a seat in the adjoining dining room. I didn't want to sit anywhere near Shelly.

"Look, Shelly, I am not sure how to explain this to you. I have moved on. I'll do whatever is necessary for the child if it's mine, but we don't have a future."

Tears began to roll down Shelly's cheeks. I expected her to throw one of her fits, but she didn't. I wasn't sure if that was good or bad. I waited for her to say something but she just sat back down and silently stared at the ceiling.

"I'm sorry Shelly."

"So you love her?"

"Yes I do, but like I said. I'll be there for my baby. That's if the baby is actually mine."

That did it. Shelly snapped and started shouting, "Stop it! Don't ever say that again." Then she lowered her voice, "I told you that baby is yours."

"Shelly, what the hell is wrong with you? You said yourself that you're almost positive that the baby was mine. What does that mean? I just want to be sure. Why do you always lose your mind when the subject comes up?" I felt like I was in another world with this girl and her actions. "I don't need this. All I want to know is if the kid is mine or not. Can you look me in my face and say without doubt that this baby is mine? Huh? Can you?"

Shelly marched over and stood directly over me in the chair.

"Brian, I said to you before that this baby is…"

A surge of rage sprang through me catapulting me into a standing position. My abrupt movement startled Shelly.

"I don't care what you said. I asked you if you could look me in my face and tell me without a doubt that this baby is mine. It's as simple as a YES or NO!"

Shelly flinched and stared at me in terror. She had never seen me this mad before. I didn't care because I was tired.

"Now I am going to ask one more time and I what to hear a yes or no. Is it mine?"

Shelly stood still. Her shocked gaze didn't waver. She hopelessly tried to blink back a fresh batch of tears. She closed her eyes giving the win to the tears. She started shaking, still not answering. I lifted her chin to make her face me.

"Please, just tell me. Is it mine?" I asked her softly.

Shelly pulled away from me, ran into her bedroom and slammed the door.

Lexie CHAPTER 33

I arrived at work an hour early to get a head start on a few major projects that were given to me during the past week. Mary Ann had also hired Shari as our new administrative assistant. When I started, Mary Ann expressed that fact that there was a need for an efficient admin to help the two of us out. Shari was the first person that came to mind. Although she was a little loud and somewhat uncouth at times, she had a huge heart and possessed the work ethic of a mule. I called to see if she was still looking for work. When she told me that she had been temping but was still looking for a full time gig, I got in touch with Mary Ann right away to get the okay.

When I called Shari back to tell her she got the job, she cried. She was bubbling and snorting all over the line.

"Thank you so much, Lexie, you won't regret this. I owe you, girl."

"Just take care of that kid of yours," I said as I silently swiped at my own tears.

Shari was due to arrive at nine to start her day and knowing her she would probably arrive by at least eight-thirty. I brought flowers and balloons to set up at her cube for a grand welcome. I knew she was going to start bubbling again so I was sure to pick up a box of Kleenex as well.

Mary Ann was in the office also as she usually started work around seven a.m., even though corporate hours were nine to five. Mary Ann came rushing over to check on the decorations at Shari's cube. I had the creative services department create a banner that read "Global Connections Welcomes Shari McDonald." From a local party store I picked up a half dozen balloons with messages ranging from, "Welcome" to "You're The Greatest." A local florist had just delivered a beautiful arrangement of tropical flowers mixed with lilies.

Mary Ann appeared nervous as if she was the one starting her first day.

"Oh Alexia, this looks wonderful. I know she is going to be so surprised." Mary Ann said as she walked around the entire cubicle admiring the set up. "Did we make reservations for lunch for the three of us?"

"I was thinking it would be good idea to have a working lunch. That way she can get all of the introductions out of the way and we can work towards helping her get acclimated as soon as possible. We're all going to be knee-deep in the grind for the next few weeks, so I have already taken the liberty of booking the small conference room on the eighth-floor and arranged for a sushi delivery. Shari loves sushi."

"Perfect, that works for me. How about we all go out for lunch somewhere on Friday? I think that will be a nice way to end her first week. What do you think?"

"I think that's a great idea. And by then she will know a little about the area and we can give her the honor of choosing the restaurant."

"Wonderful, now how are things looking on that proposal?"

Just as I was about to fill her in on my progress, I heard the ever-cheerful Shari's voice offering morning greetings to the co-workers she had yet to meet.

"Mary Ann, that's her," I whispered.

She must have walked in with someone else because reception did not open until nine and she didn't have an ID/access card yet. Mary Ann ran nervous circles around Shari's cube, making sure everything was ready. We heard Shari conversing with one of the event coordinators from my staff who was apparently showing her to her new cubicle. We stood silently waiting for her to round the end of the corridor. When she did, together Mary Ann and I yelled, "Welcome to Global Connections!"

Shari's jaw dropped to the floor along with her purse as her hands flew to cover her mouth.

"Oh my God, you guys did all of this for me? You're going to make me cry –again!"

Mary Ann and I both reached Shari at the same time and embraced in a group hug. All of our eyes had misted over at Shari's outpouring of emotion. She fanned at her tears attempting to dry them before ruining her make up.

"I told you guys you were not going to regret bringing me on board and I meant it. And knowing both of you, I know you are going to work my behind over–big time!" We all laughed.

The morning flew by and lunchtime arrived before we knew it. Shari was all set up and ready to work. Her email, voicemail, business cards and ID cards were all set up. She had even set up Mary Ann's and my calendars for the next three months. I dialed Mary Ann's extension to let her know that Shari and I would be heading down to the conference room to meet the delivery guy and we would see her as soon as she was available. During the brief elevator ride, Shari and I did a little catching up. Things were starting to really get rough for her, and our call came just in time. She was really grateful that we considered her.

Lunch had arrived and smelled delicious. The three of us absolutely loved sushi. We laid our work files on the table and hit the bags to pull out the food. I ordered California rolls, which were Shari's favorite, spicy tuna rolls and fresh yellow tail for me, and for Mary Ann, the takayama special with seaweed salad. As soon as the spread was laid, the aroma of the fresh sushi filled the room. The scent traveled to the pit of my stomach, and I was immediately overcome with a wave of nausea. I felt the color bleed from my face. Shari seemed to notice also.

"Lexie, girl, are you all right? You don't look so good."

"I think something in one of these bags was not too fresh. Don't worry about me, I'll be fine."

"Are you sure?" Shari looked worried.

"Absolutely, I'll be just fine. It's probably just the smell of that damn seaweed salad. I can't see how Mary Ann loves that stuff so much. It looks like a bowl of nasty-ass worms."

Shari let out a loud hearty laugh. I couldn't help but laugh with her. Her charm was contagious in that way.

"Should we wait for Mary Ann?" she asked.

"No, she said to get started without her and she would join us as soon as she could."

"Well good because I am hungry and I can't wait to get my fingers into those California rolls."

"I'm hungry too. Let's get a bite before we get started with any of this," I said pointing to the piles of manila folders we carried with us.

I mixed a little wasabi into my soy sauce and dipped my spicy tuna roll. Just as I popped the tuna roll into my mouth, I was overcome with a second and much stronger wave of nausea. I didn't know whether to spit the roll out or keep chewing and swallow quickly. I felt my throat close and a burning sensation rise upwards from my gut. Bile mixed with the tuna roll filled my mouth. I quickly covered my mouth searching desperately for the nearest garbage can. Shari ran and retrieved one from the far corner of the conference room. Just as she made it to me, the tuna roll, bile, this morning's buttered roll and caramel macchiato spilled through my fingers into the can. After I released everything that ever existed inside of me, I felt lightheaded.

I hadn't even realized that Shari had left the room until she came diving in with wet towels from the bathroom in tow. I cleaned myself quickly.

"I must be coming down with something."

"Alexia Mitchell, I know you are not going to sit here in front of me and act like you didn't know that you're pregnant."

I looked at Shari as if she had four heads. Pregnant?

"Shari, what are you talking about? I am not pregnant."

"Lexie, you mean you didn't know you were pregnant? I knew the moment I saw you, girl. You have always had a nice shape, but you ain't never had that much ass. And your breasts—don't they appear to be a little more voluptuous to you? They sure look it to me."

"Oh my God, Shari, you really think I am pregnant?"

"Think! Girl, I know. I have been there, remember. You might want to check that out."

Shari stretched her ear towards the door.

"Oh, I think I hear Mary Ann coming. We will pick up on this later. But I suggest you make an appointment to see your GYN—and soon."

Seconds later Mary Ann came prancing and smiling into the conference room. That Shari sure had one keen sense of hearing because I heard nothing until she was right outside of the conference room door. I quickly excused myself and ran off to the bathroom. When I returned, the three of us got right down to business. I tried my best to keep my focus but my thoughts kept wandering to the notion that I might be pregnant.

The rest of the day seemed to drag on forever. I swore everyone and everything moved in slow motion. I was anxious to get out of there, get to the nearest drug store and get my hands on one of those pregnancy tests. The thought of being pregnant both delighted me and scared the hell out of me. So many questions raced through my mind. I didn't know if I was ready for a baby. What kind of mother would I be? What about Brian? What would he say? He was already going through enough with Shelly possibly carrying his child. The timing was the worst.

At ten minutes to five I was out of the door. I didn't have the patience to wait for a train so I and hailed a taxi as soon as I reached the curb. I had to get to Brooklyn fast. I shot into the local family-owned drug store on the corner of my block and bought four boxes of pregnancy tests. I don't know why I bought so many. I guess I just wanted to be quadruple sure of the outcome.

I ran, not walked, down the block, raced into my building and flew through my front door. I flung my briefcase on the couch and raced to the bathroom. I quickly removed the first test stick from its wrapping and hung over the commode waiting for a sprinkle to descend. "Damn, damn, damn!" I turned on the faucet and ran water, hoping to influence the flow. Still nothing came.

"Come on, please!" I begged.

After a few more minutes of trying to push my bottom out, I gave in and went to the kitchen to drink a gallon of water. I was going to make sure I had enough pee to drench every test the drug store had in stock.

I stood in the kitchen tapping my fingers on the counter tops just waiting. Finally I decided to busy myself in order to try not to think about it. I picked up my briefcase and went into my room to change into a tank top and drawstring lounge pants. Then the phone rang. I peeped at the call ID and eyed Brian's cell number. I gasped and covered my mouth with my hand. I couldn't speak to him yet.

The phone continued to ring while I stood there trying to figure out what to do. If I didn't answer, he would just call my cell phone next. I snatched the phone and pressed talk before he could hang up.

"Hey there, partner." I tried to sound normal. I know I failed miserably.

Brian paused before speaking. "Hey yourself, partner. What's up?"

"Um...nothing...baby." Damn. I closed my eyes tight and stabbed at the air several times because I knew that was a dead give-away. I could believe how badly I stammered.

"You all right, Lexie?"

Suddenly the urge to pee besieged me. I yelled "YES." I could sense Brian's bewilderment through the phone.

"Ah, are you sure?"

"Huh...oh yes, babe. I'm sure. Listen, I have to go. Let me call you right back. Love you."

Without awaiting a response, I hung up on Brian and raced for the bathroom. I fumbled trying to open another pregnancy test and nearly dropped it into the toilet. I stood over the toilet doing the infamous pee-pee dance and tried to open the yet another test. My hands worked like I had five thumbs. I quickly slid my pants down and inserted the two tests into the stream of urine. Once I relieved myself and washed my hands thoroughly, I paced the bathroom watching the seconds tick away on my wrist watch for the next three minutes.

When the excruciating wait was over I picked up the sticks, closed my eyes and said a quick prayer. When I opened my eyes, two pink lines stared back at me from each test. I grabbed the box to confirm the results. Both tests were positive. I was pregnant.

That wasn't enough to make me a believer so I went ahead and took the last test. That too, came out positive. I couldn't understand how I could be pregnant when I had been on birth control for as long as I could remember. When all was said and done, three positive pregnancy tests lined my sink and I stood staring at them.

I heard a knock at my door and quickly discarded all of the evidence. I let Brian in while rubbing my sweaty palms together. I tried to think of the best way to share the news and kept coming up short. Brian looked at me with a raised brow.

"Are you okay, Lexie?"

Before I knew it I blurted. "I'm pregnant."

Brian stopped dead in his tracks and raised both brows. I didn't know whether to smile or cry. The cry won over the smile and a single tear traveled down my cheek. Brian walked over and embraced me. He kissed away my single tear, sighed then laid my head upon his chest.

Brian   CHAPTER 34

The thought of having two babies less than a year apart, from two different women haunted me. My kids would think that papa was a rolling stone. That was not the image I wanted to portray. Due to Shelly's unexpected pregnancy I had already gotten used to the concept of being a father so when Lexie told me that she was pregnant it didn't seem like such a shock. I loved Lexie to death and looked forward to making her my wife and bringing up our children together. Now that she was carrying my seed, making her my wife became a major priority.

Brooke was home now so I decided to get in touch with her and ask her assistance in finding the perfect ring for Lexie. She agreed and we decided to meet later. I was nervous, but I knew this was exactly where I wanted to be. I also had to think of a memorable way to make my proposal. I didn't want Lexie to think that I was proposing to her simply because of the pregnancy.

I hadn't heard from Shelly since she pulled her little game of false labor. She also wouldn't return any of my calls. No matter how psychotic she was, I still checked up on her to see how she progressed and make sure she didn't need anything. I suspected that the other person who could possibly have fathered this baby is the person who had been taking her to all of her visits. Perhaps, even the one who put that ring on her finger that she claimed she only wore to make me jealous.

I realized it was a few days before her due date. I called Dr. Martin to get an update on her status as I had done a few times before. I was sure she would have called me had she really gone into labor.

Roz, Dr. Martin's receptionist picked up on the first ring. "Doctor's office."

When I announced my name and requested to speak to Dr. Martin, Roz nearly cut me off mid-sentence,

"Oh Mr. Turner, Dr. Martin has been expecting your call." I was puzzled and wondered why she would expect me to call her. "Please hold and I will get her right away."

After a few short minutes Dr. Martin was on the line.

"Good morning, Brian." We had previously established a more informal dialogue. "Will you be available to come in and see me today?"

"Sure, but may I ask what this is regarding?"

"When is the last time you spoke with Ms. Winston?"

"It's been about a week. Is there something you want to tell me?"

"Brian, let me save you a trip. Shelly had the baby about four days ago."

"I thought she was due on the sixteenth. It's only the tenth."

"That's correct, but remember, I told you the baby could come before or after the due date?

"Oh, yes. I remember. I guess I can go see her in the hospital. When can I come in for my blood work for the paternity testing?"

"Well, Brian, there's a problem. There is no need for you to take your test because Ms. Winston has refused testing for the infant."

Things were starting to come together and my head began to pound.

"Exactly what are you saying doctor?"

"We cannot complete any blood work for the paternity tests without the mother's consent and Shelly refused. Until she does give consent, there is no way for us to legally test the infant in order to prove paternity. I am sorry Brian but my hands are tied. I would suggest you contact Ms. Winston directly and talk to her. I know she can be difficult at times but maybe you can convince her to do this. It would be in all of your best interest to settle this as early as possible."

"You mean there is nothing I can do?"

"I'm sorry Brian," Dr. Martin said.

"I'm sorry too. Thank you for everything."

After long pause Dr. Martin said, "Brian."

"Yes?"

"There may be one way. I would suggest you consult a lawyer."

"Thanks."

"Try to have a good day Brian, and feel free to call me if you have any questions."

I barely remember hanging up the phone. I was stunned. I wore out my floors pacing and thinking. I called Shelly's house and this time received a recording saying that the telephone number had been disconnected. I tried her cell phone but another party picked up and expressed that I had the wrong number. This chick was really playing games. Then I chuckled as I thought, 'well she said it's all or nothing.' The problem was I refused to just let this go. I could not go on in life wondering if I have a kid out there or not. I had to get to the bottom of this and quick.

I called the hospital just in case she was still there. I was informed that she had checked out two days ago with a little baby boy. A boy! I might have a son. I wondered what she named him and what he looked like. I wondered who was there with her as she gave birth. All of this really had my mind going. I was pretty messed up. I paced some more and thought about my next move. The ring of my cell phone broke the silence that loomed over the apartment. It was Brooke. I looked at the clock and it was time for us to meet.

"Damn Brooke, I am very sorry. I had an emergency and lost track of time. Can we reschedule for another day this week. Will you be around?"

"B, please. Where is my crippled ass going? When do you want to go?

Brooke was no longer dependant on crutches but she still walked with a limp. Eventually she'll be able to walk without the limp but it would take a few more weeks.

"Thanks Brooke. I will get back to you tomorrow," I said.

"Cool. As a matter of fact, I just thought of something. I know a great jeweler. Let me call him and see what he can set up."

"Thanks Brooke. You're the bomb!"

"I am, aren't I?" Brooke said and broke out laughing.

"I'll talk to you later."

After I hung up I went back to pacing and contemplating. Shelly was obviously trying to play hard ball. All I cared about was finding out if baby boy belonged to me.

I got dressed and drove over to Shelly's place. I knocked on the door like police with a search party and warrant. My knocks echoed throughout the apartment. I was sure she was gone, yet I needed confirmation. I knocked on several of her neighbors doors until someone answered and confirmed for me that Shelly no longer lived there. I wanted to hit something and could practically envision my hands around her trifling neck.

I thought about going to talk to her parents and changed my mind. As trifling as Shelly was, I didn't feel right about dragging her parents into the ordeal. Besides I wasn't sure how much of this whole thing they actually knew about. I retired my efforts for the afternoon.

For the remainder of the day I thought about the baby. I needed to know if he was mine. I also wondered where Shelly could have run off to. Somehow I would find her, but how long would it take?

The morning sun peeking through my blinds annoyed me. I barely slept all night thinking about Shelly and the baby. Brooke called me bright and early to tell me that she got in touch with the jeweler, and asked what time I wanted to meet. I really wasn't up to it but didn't want to put it off. Besides, I needed a distraction. We arranged to meet near the store later that evening.

The jeweler was located on Madison Avenue. Harvey, the shop owner was expecting us. When we arrived, he ushered us in and locked the door behind us. We exchanged greetings and Harvey told us to follow him in the back. To my surprise, he wasn't the arrogant, flamboyantly dressed jeweler that I expected. Instead he wore a simple white Hanes t-shirt, a pair of faded jeans and black moccasins. He spoke with an accent and appeared to be a very humble and pleasant man.

Brooke had already provided Harvey with a description of what she knew Lexie would love, which included something slightly understated and simple, yet elegant. To me this translated into expensive. Harvey presented us with three designs. The first was an emerald cut solitaire set in a brushed platinum setting. The second choice was an elegant radiant cut diamond with tapered baguette accents. The final choice was the one that took Brooke's breath away. It was also the most expensive of the three, but from the moment I saw the three-stone masterpiece I knew it was the one. This remarkable work of art featured a heart-shaped center stone flanked by triangular stones. The three stones represented the past, present and future.

Brooke and I exchanged knowing glances and finished our business with Harvey. Brooke was so excited you would have thought it was her who was getting engaged. The ring would be ready in two days allowing me time to think of the perfect way to propose.

I asked Brooke if she wanted to get a bite to eat before heading home and she agreed.

"So Brooke, how do I propose?"

"Let's see. You have two days to pick up the ring. In the meantime we can think of something spectacular." Brooke placed a forkful of her rotisserie chicken in her mouth. "And by the way, I couldn't be happier about you marrying my girl but you better take good care of her. I don't want to have to pull a Matrix on you." Brooke moved her hand's like Neo from the Matrix dodging bullets.

"I've got it."

"What are you thinking?"

"I know how I'm going to propose to her" Brooke's eyes widened and she put her fork down to give me her undivided attention.

"We met in a club in L.A. while we were both away on business. I want to propose to her in same club where we met."

"That's a great idea. But there is one problem."

"What is that?"

"I want to be there!"

"Get a ticket and you can. It can all be part of the surprise. I will tell her that we are going to a little weekend getaway to celebrate the baby."

"When?"

"Next weekend."

"And how are we supposed to get tickets by next weekend? You know how much that will cost?"

"Well, what am I supposed to do then?"

"Give me some time. I will come up with something," Brooke said. After a few minutes Brooke said. "What about Atlantic City?"

I raised my eyebrows. "Not a bad idea."

"Perfect. Once you propose we can all pop up and surprise her."

Brooke and I planned the weekend. Later that day I called Jeff to invite him as well. I also told him about Shelly's disappearance and the baby. He offered to treat me to a round of well-deserved drinks.

Lexie   CHAPTER 35

After the pregnancy test my doctor ordered a blood test to confirm the results and scheduled an appointment for an early sonogram. Brian and I arrived at the office a half hour early simply because we were so anxious. I was afraid of how Brian would take this because of what he was going through with Shelly. Ultimately neither of us was really ready for a baby but we welcomed the concept just the same. It still boggled me how I ended up pregnant while on the pill. My doctor reminded me of that one percent chance.

211

I was nervous about telling my parents, Dionne, Ava and Brooke. Brooke already expressed how spoiled rotten her godchild was going to be. A diva if it's a girl and surely a player if it was a boy. She helped me put my blessings in perspective and I came to grips with my pregnancy.

Brian has been spoiling me to no end. Things were still a little weird but we were going to make it. The doctor called my name and Brian and I proceeded through the waiting room into the examination area. The nurse told me to undress from the waist down and take a seat on the table. The physician's assistant, an older black woman with an English-Caribbean accent, entered the room and greeted us. Her tone was soothing and pleasant. She introduced herself and informed us that she would be performing the sonogram and that Dr. Chasen would be joining us shortly after.

Dionne wanted me to go to the infamous Dr. Martin but when I learned that she was also Shelly's doctor, I ruled that out immediately. Dr. Chasen came highly recommended and would do just fine. Andrea, the physician's assistant, asked if we had any questions as she prepared for the sonogram. She punched in some information and stated that I was nine weeks pregnant. I counted right back to the trip.

She placed a condom over the long white stick that was connected to the sonogram machine. After placing a blue gel on the top, she inserted the instrument inside of me. The cool feeling of the gel and the discomfort caused by the probing stick created a weird sensation. Andrea probed trying to capture a good view of the baby. A concerned look crossed Andrea's face.

"Is everything okay?" I asked.

"Well Ms. Mitchell, something doesn't seem to be right. If you will excuse me I would like to get Dr. Chasen in here to take a look at this sonogram." Andrea quickly exited the room to retrieve the doctor.

The panic I felt must have registered across my face because Brian immediately walked over and took my hand. Andrea quickly returned with Dr. Chasen.

"Hello, Ms. Mitchell. How are we doing today?"

"I was fine when I walked in, but now I am not so sure. Is everything okay with my baby?"

"Let me take a look here. Andrea tells me that she's not seeing the baby."

The doctor replaced the condom with a fresh one and more gel before inserting the probing instrument back into me. She printed a few shots of whatever was displayed in the monitor. After a few more minutes of poking and probing Dr. Chasen sighed.

"Ms. Mitchell, you may get dressed now. I would like to discuss this with the two of you in my office."

I didn't like the sound of this one bit and started wailing as soon as Andrea and Dr. Chasen exited the room. Brian just held me until I regained my composure.

"Brian, something is wrong with our baby."

Brian didn't speak but I could see the pain across his face. I dressed quickly and we joined Andrea and Dr. Chasen in her office.

"Alexia darling, I am afraid that this will not be a successful pregnancy for you."

I tried to blink back the tears and focus on the words coming out of Dr. Chasen's mouth. She explained that although my body was developing as it should in a normal pregnancy, the baby wasn't developing. In fact, the sac was empty indicating that there was no baby at all. She assured that there was nothing that I had done to cause this. She wanted to schedule me for something called a dilation and curettage, more commonly known as a D&C.

"Isn't there something that can be done?" I pleaded.

"I am sorry Alexia. You are at a great risk of miscarrying very soon. With the D&C we clear the uterus so that you won't have to experience the physical and emotion pain and discomfort of a miscarriage," Dr. Chasen paused.

I think she wanted to give me a moment to absorb everything. My head felt as though it had been detached from by body. By now my tears began a steady flow and blurred my vision.

"You could go for a second opinion but I wouldn't waste too much time. You are young and the sooner you take care of this the sooner you can go home and try again," Dr. Chasen said, offering a comforting smile but nothing could soothe what I felt.

Dr. Chasen showed the pictures she printed from monitor revealing a large but empty, odd-shaped sac. I turned away from the pictures and broke down.

"Oh my God! My baby!" I felt my body shaking.

Brian knelt down beside my chair and held my hands in his. I covered my face and cried into my hands. Everyone sat quietly without interrupting my downpour.

"Alexia, I understand exactly how you feel. I have been there myself," Dr Chasen said then turned her attention to Brian and whispered. "Here is my number. Take her home and let her rest. Call me tomorrow morning and we can set up the appointment for the D&C."

Brian thanked Dr. Chasen and assured her that we would be in touch the next day. He practically dragged me out of the office because my knees gave out on me. I cried all the way home and continued to cry until tears would no longer fall. Brian walked me to my room undressed me and laid me down. He went into the kitchen to fix me a cup of tea and placed in on top of my bedside table.

Neither of us uttered a single word since we left Dr. Chasen's office. The day was far from ending but I was ready for bed. I had no energy for anything else. I lay in my bed staring at the ceiling and holding my stomach. Why did that have to happen to me? What had I done wrong?

By the time Brian came for bed I was balled up in a fetal position still whimpering. Brian climbed into bed with me and cradled my body with his, laying his hands on my empty stomach. We lay together draped in a deep sense of loss until sleep carried us away.

Brian   CHAPTER 36

It turned out that the timing for the proposal wasn't so perfect. Lexie's procedure was scheduled for the day we arranged to leave for Atlantic City and then she would need at a few days to rest. The trip was postponed. Lexie sulked and cried up until the day of her D&C.

Having the procedure appeared to help Lexie come to terms with the whole ordeal. By the following day she had begun to come around and appeared to have accepted the loss. I was still dealing with it myself. I figured the surprise trip and proposal would be a great way to help both of us move on. There was still the situation with Shelly, but I wasn't going to let that stand in the way of Lexie and my life together.

I spoke with Brooke and rescheduled everything for the following weekend, which happened to be the weekend before Thanksgiving. Timing was perfect and I was anxious about the trip we planned. This was just the thing that Lexie and I needed to get our minds off of our loss and out of the emotional rut that we had settled into for the past few days. I was especially down about the fact that I had actually lost two children in a matter of weeks. Although I wasn't sure that Shelly's baby was actually mine, I felt a loss for not knowing and not being able to do anything to find out.

The day of the trip Brooke and I met at Lexie's house to pack a bag for her. Brooke had a set of keys to Lexie's place and helped me with all the details. Jeff agreed to join us. By noon Brooke, Lexie and I were packed and ready to go. Jeff had contacted the folks he knew at a club in Atlantic City to get things moving there.

Lexie called me to talk but I had to get off the phone with her to keep from blowing the surprise. I told her that I was really busy and would come by and see her later. She got upset and hung up on me.

When I arrived at Lexie's house that night the setting was perfect for me to spring my 'spontaneous' suggestion. Lexie had a full-blown attitude. She was ranting on about how I couldn't even take the time to talk to her today despite knowing what she was going through over the past week. When she realized that I wasn't going to argue back she shut down. That was my cue.

"Babe, calm down. You know I have this project to complete within a tight deadline. I know you are stressed about the situation with the baby. How do you think I feel?"

"All right, Brian. I'm just stressed," Lexie said and started pacing.

"I have an idea. How about we take a little vacation?"

Lexie stopped pacing and sat on the couch beside me, resting her hand on the back of my neck.

"When? And where to?" she asked.

"How about now?"

"Now?" she quizzed, looking puzzled.

"Yes, now," I said.

Lexie looked at me like I was crazy.

"Come on babe. Let's be spontaneous. We need it right now more than anything, right?"

"Brian, where can we go right now?" she asked shaking her

head. "How about we drive to Atlantic City?" she offered getting excited.

What the hell made her say that? Did she know? I tried not to show my thoughts. I pretended to think. There is no way she could have known.

"You know what Lexie, that's not a bad idea. Let's go," I said

"You are too much Brian. How long do you want to stay?"

"The whole weekend," I said.

Lexie started bouncing around like an excited child.

"Okay let me pack."

"No!" I shouted, just a little too fast. Lexie gave me a puzzled look. "I mean. Let's just roll. If we need something we will get it there. Just put on something cute for the ride."

"Spontaneity, I like it. You know partner, this just might work."

"Cool, let me go check out a few things and I will be back in an hour. Get ready to go."

Lexie continued jumping up and down like a kid with a new toy and kissed me goodbye. I simply went outside to call everyone and let them know that Lexie took the spontaneous angle like a charm. A half hour passed and a delivery guy from a local florist arrived with a special arrangement for Lexie and a note attached that read: "Get ready for a weekend of adventure." That was Brooke's idea.

I made a few more calls to waste time, including calling my mother to let her in on the whole plan. She gave me her blessing and made me promise to come straight to her house when we got back home on Sunday evening. She decided to prepare a special dinner to celebrate our engagement. Knowing Lexie would probably want to make her own mother's house her first stop, I told my mom I would let her know. She understood and reminded me that next week was Thanksgiving.

I went back inside Lexie's apartment, acting as if I had just come back. She gave me a sly smile as she commented on the recent delivery.

"You think you are so slick don't you. Thank you, baby," She said hugging my neck.

She kissed me passionately. I didn't want to let her go.

"All right baby, are you ready? We have to be out of here by ten. If you have any last minute calls to make or anything to take care of, do it now."

"I'm ready. Let's go!" she screamed.

Her excitement was intoxicating. She grabbed a jacket and her purse. We stopped for something to eat. She tried calling her sisters and Brooke to tell them about the surprise trip but no one would answer their phones.

Throughout the entire ride Lexie never stopped smiling. I was glad to have been responsible for putting that smile on her face. She'd been through so much these past few months.

We arrived at the hotel around two in the morning. After a few hours of sleep mixed in with a little love making here and there we set out for a day out on the town. Because of Brooke, I was left to do nothing but hang out with Lexie all day. We started with breakfast at Trump Palace then headed over to the mall to shop for outfits for the evening. After a quick lunch we returned to our room.

When we opened the door to our suite the aroma and glimmer of scented candles filled the atmosphere. The bag Brooke packed for Lexie was on top of the side table. Lexie was in awe.

"Brian, how did you get this past me? What a wonderful

surprise."

We turned on the radio and the sounds of soft jazz radiated throughout the suite. We drank champagne and enjoyed each other's company until it was time to get dressed for the club.

Lexie picked out an ivory pleated mini skirt with a matching halter that tied around her waist. She complimented her outfit with a pair of bronze pumps and matching purse. Lexie released her wrap and placed a part in the center of her hair. Her healthy straight tresses framed the sides of her face. She looked good. I threw on a simple pair of slacks with a silk button down shirt and we headed off to the club which was located about 15 minutes away from the strip.

Once inside, Brooke and Jeff made their presence known without revealing themselves to Lexie. I led her to the bar to sit and have a drink. I ordered white wine for Lexie and a Hennessey and Coke for myself.

"Brian, this is just what we needed. You know we haven't been to a club together since the night we met?"

"Yeah I remember how drunk you were." I teased. She playfully slapped me on my arm.

"Wow that seemed like so long ago."

The DJ threw on 'Step in The Name of Love' by R. Kelly. The entire crowd got hyped and Lexie pulled me on the floor.

"Come on, partner. Show me what you've got."

"What? You know you can't touch this," I said and faked a MC Hammer move.

"Oh no partner, if you're going to dance Hammer style, I'll have to pass."

Lexie acted as though she was going back to the bar. I pulled her to me and wrapped her into my arms.

"If you're with me, then you have to accept my Hammer moves," I said.

Lexie glowed when she smiled at me. We danced for the next three songs and then it was time for the festivities. The DJ announced that there was something very special for tonight and asked everyone to leave the floor except Lexie and Brian. When Lexie heard the DJ address us by name she was shocked.

"Brian, what is going on here?"

I didn't answer. The crowd dispersed and lined themselves along the edge of the dance floor. I moved to the center of the floor with Lexie in my arms as the DJ started playing "Spend My Life With You," by Eric Benet and Tamia. The music filled the room. As Eric sang, I serenaded Lexie along with him. Lexie joined me and we danced and sang to one another. The entire crowd was absorbed in the moment. Lexie never noticed when Brooke and Jeff moved to the forefront of the crowd around us.

As Eric and Tamia brought the song to a close crooning, "Spend my life with you...," I dropped to one knee and pulled the ring from my pocket. Lexie's hands flew to her mouth and tears began to fall from her eyes. She started shaking. The DJ turned the music to a soft hum and the crowd grew silent. I was nervous but refused to let anyone see me sweat. I took Lexie's hand in mine and mimicked the words of the song.

"I want to spend my life with you," and proceeded to ask, "Lexie, will you be my wife?"

Crying, Lexie dropped to her knees with me and cupped my face in her tender hands.

"Yes," she said through the tears.

The crowd applauded. On bended knee, we kissed and everything and everyone around us disappeared.

Brooke stood behind Lexie and Jeff walked up and stood behind me. Brooke placed a hand on Lexie's shoulder. Lexie turned around stunned and stood to embrace Brooke. Jeff gave me a pound and a man's embrace. The DJ announced that it was time to get this party started and threw on "Crazy in Love," by Beyonce. The crowd roared and filled the dance floor. Strangers stopped to congratulate and wish us well. After a few more dances we all headed back to the hotel to hang out in the casino. Everyone loved Lexie's ring. She was smitten by it and assured me there was none better in the entire world.

We invited Brooke and Jeff to our room to hang out but they refused. They told us that this was our night and we should enjoy it alone. We agreed to meet in the lobby the next morning at eight to have breakfast. When Lexie and I reached our room, the 'do not disturb' sign was already hanging from the knob. This time when we opened the door, the only illumination in the entire suite came from the soft flickers of countless candles. Soft music was already cued up and playing in the background. I lifted Lexie into my arms and carried her along the path of rose petals leading to the California king-sized bed. I laid her down, undressed her slowly and made passionate love to my fiancé all night long.

Lexie   CHAPTER 37

Mountain highs and valley lows were the ultimate theme of my existence. I watched the love of my life mingle with my family just after Thanksgiving dinner. I couldn't help but reflect on the highs and lows of just the past few weeks alone. I was completely distraught at the loss of my baby yet Brian turned everything around with his spur of the moment trip and proposal. He was the best thing that had ever happened to me and I was determined not to let my expectations of the worst ruin what we had. With Brian in my life, the lows didn't seem so low. Or maybe it was just my new outlook on life. I no longer looked to the next low but enjoyed the moment. I lived by Dionne's advice 'you gotta take the good with the bad. Enjoy the good, and deal with the bad as it comes.'

"You okay baby?" My mother asked as she approached me from behind.

"Yes ma'am," I turned to face my wise and beautiful mother. I could easily see where I got my high cheekbones.

"Well come on and have fun with the rest of us. And I meant to compliment you on Brian. He is a real cutie, girl. If I were about thirty years younger you would have some fierce competition!" My mother threw her thick head of hair back and enjoyed a hearty laugh.

After the engagement my mother insisted we invite Brian's mother over for Thanksgiving dinner. His mom gracefully accepted but insisted she bring a few dishes of her own.

When I looked around at all the people I loved so dearly, it filled my heart. But most importantly, I couldn't wait to get my new fiancé home and show him how much he meant to me. Brian caught me staring at him and winked at me. I felt the muscles within my vaginal walls spasm. I thought to myself, 'it's on tonight partner.' I looked around to make sure no one was looking and licked my tongue seductively, then nodded towards the door. He smiled and rolled his eyes into his head.

The festivities were coming to a close as everyone prepared to leave. After we all lent a hand to clean up the place, Brian and I offered to drop Brooke at home. She told us not to bother because Dr. Feel-Good would arrive shortly to pick her up. That left Brian and I home-free. Although I was extremely tired from all of the day's preparations, I eagerly anticipated getting Brian in the sack. As soon as we got in the car I started in on him. I lifted his sweater and fingered his chest while nibbling on his ear as he drove. I teased his thighs getting dangerously close to his middle. I could hear the tension build in his breath while his manhood grew between his legs.

Brian drove as fast as he could without blatantly breaking any traffic laws. By the time we reached my apartment, I had Brian's zipper down massaging his manhood in my warm hands. Brian carelessly threw the car into park. He fixed himself up enough to get out, grabbed me from my side of the car and raced to the building. We cackled all throughout the halls as I fumbled for my keys to make a smooth entry. An envelope taped to my door stopped me in my tracks. It wasn't addressed to anyone, which further piqued my curiosity. Brian and I looked at one another puzzled as I ripped the envelope open and found a letter addressed to Brian. I looked at him quizzically.

"Let's at least go inside," he said.

We entered the apartment and headed for the couch. I knew that the letter was from none other than Shelly. He knew as well, yet neither of us acknowledged it. I flopped down on the couch and handed the letter to Brian. As he read the letter I could see the tension build in his jaw. His eyes grew smaller and he began to bite on his bottom lip. I could only imagine what it said. When he was done, Brian huffed, handed the letter to me and paced the living area furiously.

I wasn't sure if I wanted to know what was in it but curiosity got the best of me. I figured what more could there be, so I read.

Hi Brian,

I knew I could find you here. I know you are wondering what is going on and why I refused to allow the blood test. The truth is that I am not ready for the truth myself. There are things that I can't explain to you right now. Someday I will. I am sorry, but you have to realize you hurt me as well.

I wanted nothing more than for us to be together from the very beginning. I thought for sure that when you found out about me being pregnant you would be with me and together we would be one big happy beautiful family. When I couldn't convince you to see things my way, it was hard to allow you into my life under such restricted terms. I told you I wanted all or nothing.

Someday soon I will be able to share with you the entire circumstances surrounding the baby and my disappearance. Trust me this was not easy to deal with. But until the time is right we will all just have to deal with it, won't we? I know you Brian, and I know that this may not sit well with you, but in time this will all be over and I only hope that you will understand.

Love always,
Shelly

Brian CHAPTER 3 8

I jumped out of bed startling Lexie. She sat up. The idea came to me in my sleep. I knew what to do to get to Shelly and find out if that baby was mine or not.

"What's wrong, Brian," Lexie asked angling her head towards the clock.

"Nothing, babe. Go back to sleep."

I got out of bed and started looking for my clothes. It was Monday and I had spent Thanksgiving weekend at Lexie's place.

"What time is it anyway?" she asked rubbing her sleepy eyes.

"About a quarter to five."

Without giving her a chance to say anything else I left. When I got home I took my shower and called Jeff.

"Hello," a sleepy female voice answered. It was Lena, Jeff girl-friend. This was same girl that cooked for us when we watched the game at Jeff's house.

"Hey, sorry to wake you Lena. Can I speak to Jeff? It's impor-tant."

"Okay, hold on."

She had a pleasant voice. I could hear her calling Jeff to get him up. Jeff was never easy to wake. After a few minutes, he was on the line.

"Yeah," he said in a gruff voice.

"You ate a frog last night or something," I joked.

"What you want this time of the morning?" he asked and let out a weak chuckle.

"I know what to do about Shelly."

"What's up?" I could hear Jeff perk up.

"This came to me in my sleep. I remembered Shelly's doctor saying something about speaking to a lawyer. I don't know why I didn't think of that before."

From the sound of the ruffling I knew Jeff was getting out of bed. Then I heard a door close. I assumed he was respecting my privacy since his girlfriend was lying next to him.

"Hey, my cousin Trina works at the family court downtown. I bet she could help you out too. Let me call her and see what she says."

"That's what I'm talking about. Call her this morning and ask her if I can call her or come down and see her."

"All right, I'll get back at you," Jeff said and hung up.

It was still early and I couldn't call anyone else without getting cursed out, so I went out to get some breakfast and waste time. Jeff called me on my cell at exactly nine o'clock and gave me his cousin's cell phone number. I called Trina, and asked if I could see her. She told me that she takes lunch at noon and we agreed to meet then.

Trina and I ate lunch at a nearby Jamaican restaurant. I told her my story and she advised me of my options. She urged me to go through a lawyer if I could. The process takes a while through family court, but would go much faster with the assistance of an attorney, especially if I wasn't sure of where Shelly was residing these days. She offered a few references. After lunch I went straight home and started contacting the attorneys.

The first two were out of the office. The third, Arthur Jackson, was available to speak with me. I gave him a brief overview of what I was dealing with and asked if he was available to see me this afternoon. He told me to come on over.

The storefront office was quaint but dusty. I was greeted by a young, voluptuous receptionist with a high pony tail and long colorful fingernails. Her slanted eyes smiled at me.

"How can I help you today?" she asked in a pleasant tone.

"Hi, I have a three o'clock appointment with Mr. Jackson."

"Sure. Have a seat and he'll be right out."

I took a seat on a dingy vinyl chair and waited while the receptionist got up from her position and disappeared through a beige door. I began to read the plaques and awards that lined the walls. This man was obviously well connected despite the look of his office. The receptionist returned and approached me.

"You may follow me, sir."

I followed her down the short corridor leading to Mr. Jackson's office where degrees and more plaques adorned brown paneled walls. Behind a grand cherry desk, Mr. Jackson sat talking on the phone. He stood and offered me his hand. We shook. He motioned for me to have a seat and held up his index finger to indicate that he wouldn't be much longer.

"Yes, with that we are all set...You're welcome. Talk to you soon," he said into the phone and hung up.

Mr. Jackson came around from his desk to offer a proper greeting. He was a tall black gentleman, who looked to be in his late fifties, with a pot belly and closely cut salt and pepper hair. I stood to return his greeting.

"Good afternoon, Mr. Turner," he bellowed and offered me his hand.

"Good afternoon to you, Mr. Jackson, and thank you for seeing me on such short notice."

"Arthur, please call me Arthur," he offered.

"Sure, and feel free to call me Brian, Sir."

We took our respective seats.

"What can I do for you today, Brian?"

I explained my ordeal while Arthur listened intently, occasionally taking notes on a legal pad.

"We'll get to the bottom of this, but I need you to understand one thing," he said.

"What's that?"

"It may take a little time since we need to find her first. Once we do, we can serve her and get a date scheduled for testing. Upon completion of the DNA test, we can have your results in about a week."

"That soon?"

"Yes."

"That's good to hear. I thought something like this would take months."

I gave him all of the information I could about Shelly, in order to help find her. We finalized the necessary paper work and discussed fees. I would have paid any price to get past this situation.

"Okay, Brian, just sign here and we are ready to move. I'll give you a call as soon as we have more information on Ms. Winston's whereabouts."

By the time I left Arthur's office, I felt like a huge boulder had been lifted from my shoulders. I called Lexie at work and asked if she wanted to go out to dinner. She said she was tired and preferred if we picked up a little something and ate at her place. That was fine by me, besides I hadn't gotten any work done all day. Next, I called Jeff to let him know how the day went.

The following Monday, I received a call from Arthur while I was on my way to the mall to do some early Christmas shopping.

"Good news, Brian. We have located Ms. Winston. Actually, she's now Mrs. Cabrini"

"Cabrini?"

"Yes, apparently she's married. We have her residing in Nassau County. Our office has already forwarded the necessary documents to get this thing moving."

"Thanks, Arthur that's great news. How long will it be before I can expect to hear from you again?" I asked.

"As soon as I get confirmation on the baby's testing date. In the meantime I would suggest you schedule your appointment with our DNA Counselor.

"Thanks, again. I will take care of that right away. Do you have a number for me?"

Arthur gave me the information for his recommended DNA counselor. I couldn't believe I was so close to getting to the bottom of this. I called and scheduled my appointment for later in the week. Shelly was married. I guess that's why she disappeared. What was her reason for chasing me? Where did this husband of hers come from?

I rose early that Saturday morning to get a workout in before catching up with Lexie. As soon as I got started my cell phone rang. The display read, 'Blocked Call.' Usually I would let these calls go straight to the voicemail, but I decided to be generous and answer.

"Brian!" an angry female whispered.

"Shelly?"

There was a long pause. Then I heard more whispering.

"Why, Brian? Just tell me why."

"Why do you think?"

I finally had the upper hand and was willing to take advantage of it.

"You don't realize what you are doing to me."

"And why should I care. You didn't seem to care that you've had me stringing along for the past couple of weeks. What, you don't want your husband to know?"

"My husband?" she stammered. "How did you know?"

"Never mind, how I know. What do you want?" I asked.

"I'm not ready for this, Brian. Please…"

"Well, that's just too bad. We've played this game your way long enough."

I hit the end button and got back to my workout.

Christmas was approaching way too soon. I had two days to finish my shopping. My attempts to get everything done early failed. My mind had been everywhere else. Lexie had finally arrived so that we could finish our shopping together.

When I opened the door, Lexie looked striking as always.

"You ready partner? She asked and pouted her glossy lips for a kiss.

"Let's go."

On my way out I decided to check the mail. Whenever I went out with Lexie, there was always a chance that I wouldn't make it back home that evening. As I sifted through the mail I took note of bills, bills and more bills. One envelope stood out from the rest. I felt my heart sink and a lump rise in my throat. The return address displayed the name of my DNA counselor. Unable to open the letter I handed it to Lexie. She looked at me with a raised brow then read the outside of the envelope. A look of apprehension spread across her face.

"Just open it," I nearly yelled.

"Are you sure you want *me* to do this Brian?"

"Yes. Please, just open it and tell me what the deal is."

Lexie sighed and carefully opened the envelope. I watched her skimming through the contents of the page, attempting to find the weighted information. I knew she came across the words that would determine my fate when her expression changed. She stretched her eyes and gnawed her bottom lip as she continued reading.

"What's the verdict?" I asked, not really wanting to hear the answer.

Lexie's hands fell to her side. She looked towards the ceiling and blinked away an onset of tears. My heart stopped beating then commenced to climb through my chest rapidly. Lexie sighed again.

"The baby's yours Brian."

I stood still. Nothing moved until I felt Lexie's embrace. I managed to move my hands around her body, hanging on to the rhythm of her breath. I was in limbo and didn't know what or how to feel. Lexie pulled away first, wiping the tears from her eyes. Together we silently left the building hand in hand.

THE END

Quick Order Form

Online orders: Visit **www.aspicomm.com.**

Fax orders: Send completed form to (516) 489-1199.

Postal orders: Mail completed form to Aspicomm Books, PO Box 1212, Baldwin, NY 11510.

Name: _____

Address: _____

City: _____

State: _____

Zip: _____

Daytime phone: _____

Alternate phone: _____

Email: _____

Please send _____ copies of **Mountain High, Valley Low** at $14.95 ($19.95 CAN) each plus shipping and tax where applicable.

Payment Method
Cashiers Check ❏   Money Order ❏

Credit card: MasterCard ❏   Visa ❏

Credit card number _____

Expiration date_____

Name on card _____

Signature _____

Shipping: $4.00 per book. Allow 2 to 4 weeks for delivery.

Sales Tax: Add 8.5% tax for books shipped to New York addresses.

Total enclosed: $_____